# Belt Cops

Andy Perry

To Lucy, and everyone I ever made laugh.

## Chapter 1

Cooper peered through the airlock viewport, the light from the other side illuminating his creased, stubbled, and overwhelmingly unhappy features.

"I still say we pump narco gas in," he said.

"That's your solution to everything," I replied, as I scanned the local message boards for some clue as to why the inhabitants of rotary station 324B had started rioting some eleven hours ago. One call for help had come out, but nothing since, and nobody was picking up the phone.

"It's a perfectly valid response to the tactical situation, and I reject that accusation. I'm actually quite hurt," he sniffed.

I looked up from my pad. "You suggested it last night."

"The situation…"

"As a way of getting out of paying your bar tab at the Grotbox."

He turned his back to the airlock and folded his arms.

"You're just too much of a people person, that's your problem Jimbo," he said, "always with the *let's talk about this calmly* and *I'm sure we can work this out without violence* bollocks."

He inspected a fingernail, found it lacking, and inserted it into a nostril to remedy the situation.

"Guilty as charged," I sighed as I locked my pad. I'd gleaned nothing other than that this was one boring station, and grim with it. One among hundreds of FeNi support habitats, with workers maintaining the machinery that relentlessly ground away at the countless Iron/Nickel asteroids littering the Belt's inner orbits, then packaging up the crudely refined metal and firing it off to an amalgamation depot. Rinse and repeat.

"You see anything?"

"Nah," withdraw, inspect, flick and wipe, "just a load of

smashed-up shit."

"Oh-khay, thank you for that concise sit-rep officer Cooper. I think it's Mask and Ask time."

I pulled my goggles down, engaging the side switch that pulled them tight onto my face, and unhooked my respirator from the jangling mess of my tactical vest. Neither would give more than passing help in a decompression event, but they'd protect me against smoke, offensive aerosols, a lack of oxygen, and most contaminants. As they say; *In space, farts can kill.* Or they would, if they'd ever shared an airtight compartment with officer Desmond Cooper of Central Asset enforcement; otherwise known as 'the Belt cops'.

"Shall we, old chap?" I gestured.

"Pfff, whatever."

Des masked up with fluid movements that included flicking the safety caps off several non-lethal but highly unpleasant weapons, ranging from individual vom-stoppers, group dispersal crotch-grippers, and ending with....

"Des, is that what I think it is?"

He beamed like a parent with a high-achieving child.

"Yep, got it on Bismark station last week, Brown-n-down wide area incapacitant; not made these since 2071!"

"There's a very good reason for that, as well as the legal aspect to consider."

"You're misinformed mate, it's classed as an antique and exempt from…errr…"

"Being banned system-wide because it can, and has, caused the entire population of sizable space habitats to undergo instant, persistent, explosive diarrhoea?"

"…thus rendering said population compliant to CA enforcement officers. It's a trade classic. Especially in zero gravity. The inventor tried it on himself and jetted off so hard he broke his neck. Tragic really, so much more to give."

"Put the safety cap back on Desmond."

"We're in the line of fire here!"

"Desmond, put the safety cap back on."

We faced each other eye-to-eye for approximately seven seconds.

"Fine."

"Thank you."

"Mnerfle thank me when grumpfnucking round you snurfle hammers grumpfle…."

While trusting my partner's observation skills implicitly, I peered into the small viewport to verify what lay behind. *Yep. Bunch of smashed-up shit.*

With a glance and nod to each other, I presented my CA keyfob to the door controls and took a step back. The door beeped, clanked, hissed, clunked, and eventually did its half-retracting, half-slidey thing.

The corridor beyond was brightly lit; its walls the grimy grey that only once nice white things can be, and the floor was littered with overturned trolleys, vacuum suit components, gas canisters, food wrappers, bottles, and a variety of unidentifiable crap. We walked along slowly, Cooper watching my back."

"Wuh-ho?"

I switched my external speaker on to get around the mask.

"Hellooo? Anyone there?" I said in my best don't-want-to-spook-the-snoozing-old-person voice.

"Ne nehhh? Neh neh neh nehhhh? Would you like to attend an anger management workshop?" whined Cooper. "We've got quiche!"

I stopped in my tracks; Cooper too. "You hear that?" I said.

"Mnuh huh."

I strained to hear. It was a voice, but the words were just rhythmic babble. I began to walk towards it, hands relaxed at my side, shoulders down. An approachable, unthreatening and non-confrontational body posture.

I looked to the side and saw Cooper hunched in a shuffling combat pose, both hands wrapped around a can of XL-sized crotch-gripper, sighting over the top and sweeping arcs of fire. *I'm sure 'good cop bad cop' is supposed to be something else entirely, not literally 'empath and psychopath engage with the spacefaring people of the Belt: wot larks!'*

As we moved along the corridor, carefully stepping over the strewn contents of the station, the incessant babble still did not resolve into words. *Flabbla bunbun sabba sabba dah, DAH, managga flabbla flabbla....*

On a hunch, I opened up my pad and navigated to the environment monitor suite.

*Should have checked this the minute we came in!*

I paused while I ran a broad-spectrum diagnostic check on the station air. The airlock had given nominal readings, but as Belt cops, we often had to deal with more exotic 'contaminants'; intentional and accidental, and we carried the gear to check for pretty much anything.

*Bingo!*

"Des, they're tripping balls on Myco23."

"What? Which one's that?"

"Military, airborne spores, scrambles communication skills among other things. Basically renders troops incomprehensible and hallucinating, like, megaballs."

"Hmmm," said Cooper, eyes narrowing in professional consideration. "Have we got any empty jars on the prowler?"

"Des! You are absolutely not allowed to use it against perps you fucking maniac, It's *literally* a biological warfare agent! What's *wrong* with you?"

"Just showing initiative Jimbo, it's a trait sadly lacking in today's intake of enforcement officers in my opinion."

"Your *opinion,* Desmond, has led to five increasingly serious complaints being lodged against you for excessive use of force, which obviously reflects badly on me as your partner. You only got away with the last one on a technicality."

Again, his pride was evident.

"Technical shmechnical, that one was fireproof from the start; they couldn't touch me."

"You threw improvised maggot grenades at a picket line."

"And?"

"Of school children. Trying to get a dinner lady reinstated."

"It dispersed the gathering in a non-lethal manner and used no prohibited substances; win-win!"

"Wi...?" I repitched my voice down. "Des, those people, those *children* suffered severe psychological trauma!"

"Oh here we go again...look, we've got a job to do and..."

"Flabbalabba?"

A naked, dirty, and wild-eyed worker stood by an upturned office chair not ten feet away. *So much for situational awareness.*

"Balabbang-ibba," he said, pointing to an empty area of space.

"Yes, it is, isn't it!" I said through my best general-purpose smile.

Cooper growled and held the crotch gripper low but ready. I hoped I was out of its dispersal cone. As rookie Belt cops we all got hit with vom-stop, crotch-grip, and other non-lethals in our training, to make us realise how incredibly debilitating, unpleasant and painful they were and to discourage casual use. Cooper, obviously, thought it was the best thing *ever* and purposely flunked the module so he could go through it all again to: "You know James, really get a *feel* for it?"

"Nibboh!" said the naked, hallucinating asteroid miner.

"Mmm, yeah, I feel that way too," I opened a CA override to the station's environmental control system, "do you think it's a common problem?"

"Bim. Bim. Bimbim!" He pressed imaginary buttons made of star unicorns.

Cooper was a smoldering presence, but stable. For now.

"Well, it's understandable I suppose," *initiate fungicidal mist treatment, expedite, initiate SchizoSedate mist treatment, expedite,* "though I doubt they'd benefit in the wider scheme of things."

The naked space miner just looked at me quizzically.

"What the fuck are you talking about?" he said.

He looked down.

"Why am I naked?"

"That sir," I said, "is what we're here to find out."

Cooper grudgingly rose from his combat stance. A call without the use of weapons was no call at all for him, and I predicted a major-league grump descending. If we could find the culprit behind the Myco23 dispersal he could at least terrorise a prisoner on the trip back to the station.

"I'm officer James Byron, and this is officer Desmond Cooper of 77th sector enforcement. Can you tell us what you remember about the last few hours please sir?"

"Fuckin' Belt cops," he scowled at us before turning to stalk off up the corridor.

I sighed and considered, for just a moment, if Cooper's scorched earth policing policies were not, in fact, broadly justified.

"Let's go," I said, following the dubious beacon of a pair of jiggling arse cheeks.

## Chapter 2

"So, you called this in as a riot, is that right?"

I spoke mostly to the floor to avoid looking at the control room full of people in various states of undress, several of them jury rigging coverage, some seeming really not that bothered, though obviously perturbed by losing hours of memory. And clothes. Cooper leaned against a console, eyes roving at will and quite obviously just *loving* the discomfort in the room.

"Uh, yeah, I remember that at least."

My interviewee was the duty control room supervisor, a middle-aged woman with close-cropped red hair, currently sporting a plus-size swimsuit made of duct tape and paper plates.

"The second shift had just swapped out and the runabout was prepping to launch when I saw the canteen going off on the security monitor."

"Going off?"

"Just, everyone throwing stuff about, ripping clothes off… not really fighting as such, just…."

"Going off?"

"Yeah."

"Oh-kayy. So, any problems with drug use on the station?"

The woman visibly bristled into the physical embodiment of the words: "No comment," and "pig."

"Oh, just the usual, nothing much," she lied, airily.

"Right. It's just that Myco23 is only used, these days at least, as a recreational drug, and it's pri-tee uncommon, hard to source you see."

She remained motionless and uncommunicative.

I mirrored her lack of response and waited.

Cooper's ears sprung up at the detection of the slightest

possibility he could employ violent coercion in his duties as an enforcement officer. *Down boy, bad dog!* I sent over our cop-partner psychic bond.

Plate-bra wasn't giving in, so I added, "Of course, Myco23, being prohibited under the Geneva convention on biological weapons, moves this into much more serious legal territory."

Her eyes thinned, just a little.

"Probably cause for an Intervention Deployment."

Her eyes widened, appreciably.

The Belt by and large hates us because we spoil their sense of frontier freedom. And because we employ malevolent entities like Cooper. But it's mostly the freedom thing. An Intervention Deployment meant a permanent Belt Cop presence on the station, often consisting of officers being punished for 'not expressing the core humanitarian principles of the organisation.' Officers like Cooper, for instance.

She side-eyed my partner who gave her a *devastating* right-handed eyebrow raise.

"Hummpf, well, there is this young kid in sewage services, I forget her name, she…maybe…you should….?"

*That'll do.*

"Excellent, ident code please."

"Yeah, she err…"

"Doesn't have one. Of course."

It's hard to be accurate, but about forty to sixty per cent of what goes on in the Belt is illegal, or couldn't give a shit either way and we, as the space filth, have to negotiate this issue literally every minute we're on duty; choosing when and how to enforce, ignore and sometimes manipulate 'The Law'. All space persons were supposed to have personal, embedded ident chips that could be used in a variety of ways to encourage a cohesive, obedient, and traceable population. *Yeah, right.*

"Sewage services are on level four, subsection G; if she's

anywhere she's there."

"Thank you, you really have been most helpful." I gave her a not-entirely-artificial smile. Which visibly freaked her out even more.

"Uh, yeah," she said, scratching at a paper-clad boob.

*****

We took the scenic route through the station in order to check that everything was getting back to normal, and demonstrate, with a show of force, that CA enforcement was, despite most spacers' opinions, somewhat 'in charge' when things went non-linear.

*Yep, that's right; we are The Law, majestic and pure.*

"Do you think that spraying syrup at perps and releasing wasps would work?" Asked my sociopathic sidekick.

"I mean, you wouldn't *actually* be causing harm yourself, would you?" he continued, "It'd just be the wasps going at the perps, and they're all like, '*Arrgh, get these fucking wasps off me!*' and shit?"

He looked at me with the sincerity of a child asking why the sky is blue.

"It's worth considering," I said, knowing that he'd consider it whether I agreed or not. *We all need support and encouragement from time to time.*

"Hmmm," he nodded. "Insecticide to finish up. Nice."

A man limped by, quite obviously impeded by the fact he, or someone else, had breach-glued a variety of office items to him.

"Can I help you at all, sir?" I asked.

"Eat my shit, copper," he replied, a staple gun clacking on his kneecap as he went by.

Cooper lovingly stroked his can of Brown-n-down as he watched him go. I placed a hand gently on his arm.

"Maybe one day, Des. Maybe one day."

We found sewage services by a combination of senses, smell featuring foremost, and apprehended the suspect in the crime with classic, textbook detective work; we ran straight into her. The worried-looking young woman had beaded hair, a patchwork jumpsuit and carried an honest to god 1930's, velvet-lined cinema usher's tray, declaring: *'Ali's mobile drug emporium'* in period gold text on the front panel.

"Hello! Ali, is it?"

"Errh, no, that's…this is…"

Cooper moved effortlessly into stage one intimidation range.

"This looks like an interesting selection, what's this?" I asked, picking up a small purple bottle.

"That's…muscle relaxant, we get a lot of tense muscle injuries here. I mostly sell medicinal compounds. I'm a shamanic healer too," she smiled, quite believably.

"She-man he-her?" asked Cooper, visibly straining at the calculation.

"She said *shamanic healer*, it's a sort of spiritual doctor, isn't it, Ali?"

"Yes. That's right."

"Yes. And *sometimes* a shaman will utilise the *healing* power of psychedelic substances. I read that somewhere."

She cleared her throat.

"Are you familiar with Myco23, in your professional experience as a healer, Ali? I hear it's particularly, umm, *transformative*?"

"Look, it was an accident, I didn't…"

Cooper moved the short distance into stage two intimidation range; *'I can smell your fear.'*

In time-honoured fashion I clapped a hand, gently but

purposefully, on her shoulder.

"Ali?"

"Yes?"

"You're nicked."

"Hurr." said Cooper.

*****

It turned out that 'Ali' was in fact Alison Drexler, and at the age of seventeen no longer classed as a minor according to CA policies; rather a 'Young Adult'. This, therefore, meant that while we could still arrest and charge her with possession, intent to supply, and gross negligence endangering a space habitat, yadda yadda, we were under strict orders not to let her 'fall down the stairs'. Stairs being a rare thing in space, this was more likely to take the form of handcuffing, entering a zero-G environment, and letting inertia do the hard work; "*He flew into a bulkhead guv.*"

She'd also go through a somewhat different route from punishment or jail. It made little material difference, but 'showed willing' towards offenders not yet habituated to crime.

Cooper was particularly unhappy with the situation and was almost vibrating out of his acceleration harness with pent-up aggression. I turned around to the restraint seats where we keep prisoners in transit.

"Ali, have you got any animal sedatives in your stash?"

She opened her mouth, and then her brain caught up and closed it for her.

*I was sincerely interested,* I thought, as I watched Cooper repeatedly jabbing himself in the thigh with his *definitely* not-Belt-Cop-issue Tazer-knuckles.

I rotated my seat fully round to face her. I could hear the

tinny cacophony of *Chainsaw Aneurysm* coming from
Cooper's earbuds and decided it was safe to proceed.

"Look, Ali, I realise what you generally think of us, but I
really am one of the 'good ones', and you're in an incredible
amount of trouble here. You can start to help yourself by
helping me. Where did you get the Myco23 from?"

"I want legal representation. I'm a Young Adult and have
special rights under Belt law," she stole a glance at Cooper
and added, "especially regarding enforcement by coercion or
force."

"Well, that covers your rights under Belt law, so well done
and good for you!" I beamed at her. I'm ever so good at
beaming. Her features flickered a glimmer of hope.

"However, Myco23 is not only a prohibited substance
under the misuse of drugs act 2069, but also a prohibited
biological weapon under the 2053 Geneva convention, which
overrides the former in times of mass civil unrest or war, and
being conflict-based legislation, has far harsher terms on the
treatment and conviction of prisoners."

My kung-fu was obscure legal bollocks, and it was *strong*.

"But we're not at war!" She blurted.

"I'm pretty sure we've just witnessed a scene of mass civil
unrest though, don't you?"

"I told you, it was an *accident!* I dropped a vial near the
intake scrubbers!"

Her eyes were filling up a little. *Arrgh! Kryptonite! Work fast!*

"Look, we're not after you, really we're not, but the people
who sell this stuff are *bad people*. You don't have bio-
weaponry on your shelves if you're a friendly neighbourhood
wholefood co-operative."

"And what are they going to do to *me* when they hear I
ratted on them?"

The floodgates opened. *Oh shit....*

"James, have you just intimidated this prisoner to tears

without me?"

*Oh, shit shit shit….*

"Mnuhh, mnuhh, not my fault, mnuhh, left me on the station at eight years old, mnuhhh…"

"You duplicitous sack of fucking turds! I *knew* I should have chosen Bailey as a partner but noooo, you were all like; 'Desmond, you need someone who'…."

"Blahhhh! Had to live in a *fucking sewage tank! At eight! Blahhh…"*

"You *wanker!"*

"BLAHHHH!"

And so on and so forth.

## Chapter 3

We were about four hours from docking at sector 77 station and had flipped over to begin the deceleration burn. The prisoner was a snuffling bag of slowly congealing snot, and if resentment had density, my partner was a mid-sized black hole. Fortunately, that meant very little came out of his seething event horizon, and I was safe to orbit him (at a distance).

*'Proximity alert, proximity alert; vessel on collision course.'*
"Huh."
Given that police vessels in the Belt are constantly broadcasting their ID in normal circumstances (such as not heading to bust an unlicensed brothel) and that illegal practices are almost ubiquitous wherever we look (ditto unlicensed brothels), most ships stay out of our way. Like, at least 50,000km out of our way. One heading straight for us was…interesting.

Going on the premise that a Belt cop standard issue prowler could be (and under his control, actually *was* an offensive projectile weapon - *see complaint for use of excessive force #3*), Cooper was actually a pretty good pilot, and his fingers were dancing on the controls by the time I'd spun my seat around.

"Transponder is off, coming in from five o'clock starboard, seventy-five degrees off our course…he's turning in at 3G." He paused, eyes fixed on the long-range scan readouts. "Yep, definite intercept course, twenty-five minutes give or take."
"3G?"

"3 fucking G." He smiled. *Playdate!*
Anybody pulling those kinds of forces to arrive at our patch of space was fairly determined. I set the general ship-to-ship radio to channel sixteen and cleared my throat.

"This is CA enforcement vessel 77-14 Scamp to inbound vessel, do you require assistance? Over."

Cooper was grinning and doing something clever with the scanner, which seemed safe enough. *Aw, surprise walkies!*

"This is CA enforcement vessel 77-14 Scamp to inbound vessel, you are on a collision course. Please state your intention. Over."

Still no reply.

"Right," said Cooper, "I've got a better read off the long-range, hard to tell for sure but looks like a Krait-class skiff, sidelobes spiking quite a bit; possibly armed with kinetics or beams; could be both."

"Really?" I thought about the situation for a second.

"The fine detail range on the scanner is rated for about 5k max...how are we getting all this at 30k+?"

He did the funny little ballet of gestures and shrugs utilised only when he knew he'd *really* crossed the line, that line being so far downrange of what normal people would class as 'the line' that whatever he was covering up had to be nudging the realms of 'war atrocity'.

"What did you do, Cooper?"

"Just...boosted the power a bit, 'sall. Popped some new output tubes in. And stuff."

I considered this.

"Cooper, have you converted the ship's scanner into a death ray?"

He rubbed at a fingerprint on the console for a few seconds, then quietly said, "Yes."

"I see."

"It still works really well as a scanner at long range though!"

"Yes, I can see that. It's really quite good."

"I know, right?" *Bouncy bouncy!*

"And at short range; fries living tissue? Converts spacesuits into microwave ovens?"

I could see that the conversation was about to spill into the usual moral argument of an 'us or them' nature, and considering we had a possible real-life 'us or them' situation brewing, I held up a hand to signal the conversation was, for now, at an end.

"Got to be a merc...a ship like that; yeah?"

"Ohhh yeah," said Cooper.

We cogitated for a few seconds, arrived at the same conclusion, and looked over our shoulders at little miss narco-entrepreneur 2084.

"Looks like your bio-weapon buddies are trying to spring you," I said, getting her attention very quickly.

"But...I never even met them! I've just got a guy on the supply shuttle - I had my usual order come in and there was a box with nine vials in it, I didn't even know what it was, honestly! I just sell zinga, numnums, and prongadong mostly. I never mess with the hard stuff; the station would space me if I did!"

Having heard every variation possible on *it fell into my hand / in my pocket / up my butt etc*, I'm pretty hardened to this kind of plea of innocence, but looking at her and thinking about the whole situation, I couldn't help but bite just a little, and my cop sense was tingling.

Myco23 was *really* hard to find in a viable form, and as far as anyone knew, hadn't been manufactured since the water wars of the 2040s. The station Ali was from was grim, sure, but working grim; not pit-of-seething-depravity grim; simply not the place you'd expect to find such a niche brain-nobbling war-fungus. And Ali seemed like....just a kid hustling to survive, same as thousands of others out here. If we'd bumped into her without the Myco23-induced freak-out party, we'd probably never have arrested her; unless she'd actually tried to sell us drugs. Or tried to charge us too much.

Then I belatedly realised how many personal doses of Myco23 would fit into the eight vials I'd found in her backpack; now down in our hold. *Those were sealed mil-spec delivery vials; you could take out an army with that much gear!*

I pointed the silent finger of '*to be continued, young lady*' at her and turned back to my console.

"Options, my little dog of war."

"Hooo!" said Cooper. "Well, if we call for backup now…"

I flicked up the red protection cage and pressed the button that sent out an automated '*For the love of fuck please send backup!*' signal to any and all Belt cops in the sector.

"… despite your cowardice and complete lack of martial backbone, it'll be at least two hours before the station gets anyone here. So we're on our own," and something involving 'couscous' and 'social worker'. It was hard to make out.

"Well," I said, "we'd better get ready for company then."

"Well, durr," said Cooper.

*****

It's been a bone of contention with us for a long time, but Belt Cop ships are not armed (unless your homicidal partner takes matters into his own malign hands). There's a sound reason for this, in that the Belt as a whole only allows us to operate as 'The Law' by maintaining a margin around the outside that insulates them from having 'The Navy' in charge - or any armed force capable of actually giving them a good kicking. The reason the Navies of Earth and Mars don't hold sway in the Belt is that the Belt is *uncommonly* good at flinging asteroids and asteroid chunks around the solar system, and they have so, so, *so many* of them. Initiating a dinosaur-level extinction event would just be Tuesday for the Belt.

While there's never been a war *as such* between the Belt and inner planets, there have been periods of 'discomfort' when the fledgling Belt population, like a toddler finding that it has free will but also discovering the world has the *fucking temerity* to say things like, "please don't lick the toilet brush", has a little bit of a tantrum.

The average Belter will of course say the Belt cops are a bunch of useless shitweasels and they *don't need no steenking peegs*, but the rough patchwork of what passed for a government out here saw the need for *just a little* policing. More importantly, an outside force that they could deflect blame onto as a bunch of useless shitweasels.

While the Belt's government said '*Oh I suppose so*' to us using non-lethal force to make naughty Belters toe the line, there's no *way* they're letting us have spaceships that can actually do anything more offensive than going 'nee-nah' in space when on an emergency call. Though, space being a vacuum, we mostly make that noise ourselves on the flight deck. Really, we do.

In short, if the brass got wind of Cooper's scanner DeathMod v1.0, we were in deep space doo-doo.

\*\*\*\*\*

Our unwelcome friend was about twelve minutes out when we got a tight beam transmission on the tactical set. *How military.*

"*Listen up you pigshit pigfuckers; you've got our property and we're taking it back or taking you apart!*"

"VRAAAARRRT!" went our energy proximity alarm; a shot across the bows, probably an adapted mining laser.

"Bit rude," said Cooper.

"Yes, I thought so too."

"Ahhh! I'm going to die!" Wailed Ali.

"There's a distinct possibility!" Chirped Cooper, giving her a nice smile over his shoulder.

"This is CA enforcement vessel 77-14 Scamp to vessel closing on our position. And shooting at us. Thank you for declaring your intentions. Wasn't so hard, was it? Over."

*"Don't play smartarse with me! You've nine units of, heh, product you've stolen, and it's going to be returned or we slice you open and come find it ourselves - your choice, but make it quick. We're not patient men!"*

"This is CA enforcement vessel 77-14 Scamp to vessel containing impatient men firing at us, message received and understood. We think we know what it is you want and are pleased to tell you we're about to release a beacon-equipped vacuum canister with your, *ahem*, *product* inside. You really shouldn't fire lasers at us though. We are the police. It's literally illegal. Over."

*"Lit...? Listen, literally fucking DEAD is what you're going to be if you give us any more shit. You're locked into our targeting scanner, so no funny business, ok? Next shot takes you apart!"*

"This is CA enforcement vessel 77-14 Scamp to vessel being overly aggressive in the situation. Fair enough. Over."

I switched to the ship's internal comms; Cooper was in the hold preparing the vacuum canister. "Ok for release Des?"

"Yep, going overboard now," he replied.

I heard the clunk of the outer airlock door opening through the hull. We were still in deceleration burn, so the canister started to fall away immediately. The other ship would be in range of it within minutes, probably with a weave-grab deployed.

"Do you think they'll leave us alone when they get the drugs?" asked Ali, who I'd uncuffed but left secured in the acceleration seat; spaceships, inertia, and floppy bone bags being what they were.

"Oh, I should think so. After a fashion."

She didn't look too happy at my answer, but kept quiet about it.

Cooper opened the access hatch from the hold and gave me a happy thumbs up.

"Oh-khay. Let's see…you know your new death ray?"

"Yesss?" he said cautiously, fearing his new toy was about to go into the naughty cupboard. Seriously; he's got one.

"At the range of, oooh, say 3k, what do you think it would do if you fired it at a targeting scanner? A normal person's scanner, not, you know; 'burst the space person's eyeballs' type. Like yours."

Sharp intake of breath. "Ooooh, it'd be fucking fucked. The receiver's front end would be cheese on toast, probably take out anything not EM hardened around it too."

"Yes, I thought that may be the case." I smiled at him, and I don't know if I've ever seen a happier psychopath. *Playtime!*

"Just set it up for now Des, we wouldn't want to spook them, would we?"

"Nooo. Not that. Not ever."

"And let's see if we can't have a look at these rapscallions, eh?"

I toggled the optical follow on the general (non-incinerating) scanner and scrolled the display into the merc ship. The purposeful-looking Krait-class skiff was indeed bristling with weapons rails, twin beams, and some kinetics; probably some Belt special missiles, not to be messed with, despite their workshop origins. At the limit of zoom we could make out the flight deck windows, twin malevolently slanted oblongs, slowly growing larger as they closed on our position.

The radio burst back to life.

*"Hey piggy piggy, looks like you've half a brain cell at least mumble mumble bring it up here. Heh, shame that's all you've got 'cos if you*

*think you...what? What the fu...that sme...ca...unngh,
nrarrrgthrupppp...."*

"If you would, Desmond."

The gigawatts of microwave energy, tightly focussed onto the merc ship, caused blue flashes and shimmering waves over the hull, and a larger orange flash told of some equipment being vaporised with the overload. The whole ship began a slow tumble as the drive flares sputtered out as a bonus, and there, on the flight deck, we glimpsed figures in mid-air, suddenly caught in zero-G. Then, quite rapidly, the flight deck windows started to turn brown; the occasional impact of a face or shoulder giving an impressionistic smear to the tableau.

I turned to see Cooper wiping a tear from his eye.

"It's so beautiful. Thank you, James."

"No worries partner, I got your six. Always."

"Has anyone ever spoken to you guys about your unhealthy codependent relationship?"

"Shut up, Ali," we said, in perfect unison.

## Chapter 4

I'd stood down the emergency shout and we were about forty minutes from docking at the sector 77 CA enforcement station: home.

We were towing a spaceship full of liquid poo, several mercenaries in dire need of IV fluid infusions, and a pressing need for a backstory that would minimise the fallout we were about to encounter from, respectively, the ship maintenance guys, the duty emergency medical team, and not least, Saunders, our unit commander.

On our side was an honest to god haul of bio-weapons or narcotics (depending on which boxes needed ticking for the annual review), an illegally armed merc ship, and a flight deck record of being threatened verbally and physically with annihilation.

*Not* on our side was the fact we'd used a death ray and a very grey area non-lethal like Brown-n-down to defeat and apprehend our would-be executioners.

"It's going to be a tricky one," I said, walking back onto the flight deck from our little galley alcove with three cups of tea and a packet of McFisties digestive biscuits.

"Can't see it myself," said Cooper, stretched out and still bathing in the afterglow of deploying two high-quality weapons at once, "if *that* wasn't a situation requiring extra force then colour me confused."

I offered Ali a mug of tea off the tray and flexed a few biscuits up the wrapper for her to grab. *Kid looks like she needs a decent meal.*

"Thanks," she said, meekly.

*And what are we going to do about this one?* I thought.

"That's not the point Coop," I said, placing his *My little pony* mug on the console, "it's the fact that we were going about CA business tooled up with those things already. You know, *carrying offensive weapons in strict contravention of et cetera?*"

"Mneeeeh!" He expressed.

I just sighed and sipped my tea. *Oh blessed Brown Leaf Water, guide me in my hour of need.*

"I tipped you off," said Ali.

"What? No you didn't," replied Cooper round a mouthful of McFisties.

"No, listen - you came to the station in response to the, err, incident, and I tipped you off that the Myco23 was on the station, but that mercs were inbound to collect it, and *they* were tooled up and looking to take you out. I helped you defend yourselves in a potentially life-threatening situation by locating the can of Brown-n-down and fixing up your scanner and stuff. It'll all be on me, mostly. I take the fall and we forget my, umm, business activities?"

"Hmmmn," I said.

Cooper erupted tea and biscuit lava in indignation, "No chance! You take all the glory? Not while I'm in charge, nerrrp…."

"…and why didn't we call for reinforcements while we were on the station?"

"There were merc agents on the station, you couldn't risk tipping them off by using station comms….and your long-range ships radio was broken."

"Hah! But it's not, is it, little miss clever….."

"Desmond, smash the long-range radio."

*SMEKZZTSSS*

Cooper looked down at his sparking, Taser-knuckle equipped fist, up at the smoking ruin of the radio, and his higher brain functions caught up with whatever velociraptor-based ones that were his primary interface with the world.

"That was uncalled for, James."

"I know, and I'm genuinely sorry, but it really is for your

own good."

He slumped back into his acceleration chair, deflated.

"Sooo…about me," said Ali

"Yes, about you," I said over the rim of my mug.

"Have you got, like, protective custody and stuff?"

I choked slightly on my tea. "Not really. Question of resources, I'm told."

"Ah. Right. It's just that, I don't think I'd be very safe back on the station anymore? Or very welcome, once it gets out what caused the, um, thing."

"Hmm."

I tapped my fingernail on the mug.

"Well, whatever happens, it's going to be dependent on how our commander takes all…this. I can put in a good word, big up your part in our report, the risks you were under, but if he goes apeshit…"

"Right. Well, thanks…I mean it."

*Huh. I think she does.*

\*\*\*\*\*

I was losing track of the emotions boiling off the squat, jowly commander Saunders as he digested the report we'd delivered to his office and the poo-filled evidence locker we'd docked onto his space station.

On one hand, the haul of Myco23 was a total gift, beefing up his yearly average of narcotic *and* weapons seizures ('Nothing in the regs to say they don't both count boys!'); ditto the Krait, once it had been repaired and *very* well cleaned (minus points for the *eeew!* factor).

On the other hand, our story about Ali tipping us off and helping to source the naughty weaponry was clearly complete bollocks, (because, well, Cooper, basically) but if it passed close enough inspection to go on the official report to head office….

"So, officer Cooper. Am I to believe that you had *nothing* to do with the, *offensive measures* undertaken on this mission, and this, *young lady* was in fact largely responsible for incapacitating an armed mercenary ship and its crew?"

"Umm. Yes please? Ahhh…"

"That *is* the case, sir, though as you can see," I placed a supporting arm around his shoulders, "officer Cooper is *very* fatigued from his active role in the mission."

Turned out Ali *did* have some animal sedatives in her stash after all.

*Nearly there Coop. Oh shit; he's starting to drool….*

"I see," said the commander through steepled fingers.

*Yeah, clearly.*

"Well, congratulations on the mission outcome to all of you, and especially to your new trainee. I expect to hear great things of you in due course, Miss Drexler, though as a trainee officer you will of course have to eschew using such *violent* and *non-permissible by treaty* methods in your future work."

"Thank…what, who?" I said, as Cooper slumped further into my side. I was struggling to keep him upright. "Trainee?"

Ali just stood there, mouth ajar.

"Yes. I thought she showed *excellent* initiative in the situation!"

"Oooo!" said Cooper, raising an unsteady finger of outrage which I gently lowered for him.

"But sir, this is *very* irregular! She's not gone through any CA enforcement training at all - if she could just…"

"Ah, but it's *not* irregular officer Byron. It's actually a new scheme where Young Adults deemed 'at risk' are placed with existing partners for on-the-job training; saving us a decent wodge of cash *and* fulfilling the CA commitment to the

Youth Council Pathway initiative. You *did* stress she was at risk and should be considered for special dispensation in your *entirely accurate and truthful report* James, didn't you?"

"Ob, ob, ob…but Cooper's a fucking nutter! It'd be an unsafe educational environment!" I shrieked, desperate.

Cooper looked at me with a cross-eyed, drooly smile.

"Ish shu my da? Need poo."

"Yes James, he is. But he's your nutter, isn't he?"

"Pooooh."

\*\*\*\*\*

We managed to manhandle Cooper out of the command section, onto a porters trolley, and from there to his bedroom on ring three, where we put him into the recovery position and stuck a towel under his head for the drool.

"And the miners take this stuff for recreation, do they?" I asked, hands on hips, looking down at his boneless body.

"Mnyeah, but mostly to come down off zinga after double shifts - kinda equals it out. On its own…" she gestured at Coop.

"Hmmmn."

"Yep."

"Gnarrrrg," said Cooper, twitching slightly.

*Probably chasing rabbits.*

We spent a few seconds in awkward silence, looking around the walls at Coopers WarBastard 50,000AD posters and felt tip designs for pedestrian mowing spider tanks.

"So, like, what do we do now?" Asked Ali.

I winced at the 'we' but started to pull myself together. *Maybe this is no bad thing,* I tried to reason.

"Well, for now we'll get you something to eat, somewhere to sleep, and I'll look through this, see what the deal is."

The Captain had given me a ring binder labelled *Young Adult enforcement training: a manual,* featuring a cover picture of a laughing pair of officers, male and female, and a fresh-faced trainee putting a choke-hold on a bug-eyed, grizzled miner in a stained jumpsuit.

"Cool," she said, nodding.

"Cool," I agreed.

We turned off the light, closed the door and left Cooper snurkling on his bed. I gestured the way to the canteen.

"Sorry you got stuck with me, back there. You seemed quite upset."

I winced again.

"Don't take that the wrong way Ali, you seem like a decent person, it's just that…well, you've met Cooper; he's…special. Takes a lot of work to manage, and I just don't know how this will all…fit together yet."

She nodded and seemed to take that in.

After a while, I asked, "So, no family on the station then?"

"Nope," she scuffed at the floor as she walked, "genuine space orphan…I remember my dad, but don't know if I'd recognise him if I saw him now."

"Ah. Sorry. Tough way to grow up. You got friends though?"

"Mneh, kinda. Some people were ok, but, mostly they were just customers. Had to keep a bit of distance."

"We'd have to be careful, but if there was anyone there you needed to get a message to….?"

She thought a little, then said, "Nah. Not really."

I really wanted to give her a little hug right then and there, but I was pretty sure there was an entire chapter in the binder about not doing that, so I kept my hands to myself and led us to the canteen, where she proceeded to empty plate after plate of food. A small crowd gathered, uncertain if they were watching some kind of competitive eating wunderkind in training.

She finished the display by giving a belch that brought a round of applause from the entire canteen, including the dishwashers down the hall. *That's my trainee that is!*

We were both dead on our feet, so I took her to an unclaimed transit bunk near mine, wrote A. Drexler on the slip of card on the door, checked there were some standard-issue blankets and toiletries in there, and stood outside, hand outstretched to usher her in.

"Wow," she said, "is this really mine?"

"Well, it's yours on the station. I'll sort you out a uniform in the morning."

"Wow." She just stood looking at the tiny, plain, utilitarian room.

"Ok, get some sleep, we'll meet you in the canteen at 8:30 tomorrow for…"

She came in, hugged me, released me and shut the door behind her so quickly that I had no chance to do anything but gawp.

"You're welcome," I said quietly, and turned to find my own oblong of Belt cop home to collapse onto.

It'd been a long shift.

## Chapter 5

Ali was onto her second full English breakfast when Cooper finally stumbled into the canteen and came over to our usual table.

As he neared us his bleary eyes focused on Ali and he stopped in his tracks, swaying slightly.

"What the fuck is this snot-based life form doing here?" he said thickly, pointing at her.

"Sit down Desmond, let's get some food into you and all have…"

"Why is it wearing a uniform? In my seat?"

He looked around to check which universe he was inhabiting, found no major discrepancies and again asked, "Why?"

"Desmond, the snot-based life form is called Alison, as well you know, and…Alison is our new trainee! Isn't that nice?"

He looked at her.

He looked at me.

"No. What's happening?" He looked around again, visibly agitated that he could find no proof that he was in a particularly bad dream.

I stood up, gently led him over to the table and sat him down.

"Now, Coop. Coop-de-doop. Me old pal."

"Urrrgh. Feel like I've been sick into my brain."

He reached over, took Ali's coffee mug and poured it into his face.

"Yes, well, you started feeling a little unwell during our debrief with Saunders yesterday, probably all the excitement. And stuff."

"Debrief. Saunders. Urrrgh."

"I'm sure you're going to feel better soon."

"Urrrgh."

"And while you're recovering, I thought we could take time to welcome Alison into our little family. Yay!"

Ali gave a quiet little "Yay!" and head bob.

Cooper looked at us like we were completely insane. Which was a bit rich, even given the circumstances.

"I 'member coming off the prowler...report. Saunders..."

"Yes, we gave our report and the commander thought Ali here had *really* stepped up to the mark; showed she was a team player, and that's why she's going to be our full-time trainee for the next six months. Isn't that *nice?*"

"No, stop saying that!" He was starting to come around as the station issue coffee (refined and developed over centuries of sobering up police ready for their shift) did its work.

"Why do I feel this shit? I can't remember dri...OOOH!"

He pointed at me.

"You drugged me! Again!"

I sighed, first of the day.

"Yes Cooper, I drugged you. Actually, we both drugged you in a manner of speaking. Welcome to the new group dynamic."

"Urrrrrgh!"

"Look, If you'd gone in front of Saunders unsedated there's *no way* you'd have kept to the story; not when it came to Ali masterminding the Brown-n-down and death ray stuff."

"WAHHH! THIS IS SO UNFAIR!" howled Cooper at full tilt, head back.

The canteen barely missed a beat, animalistic howling being perfectly normal noises coming from Cooper.

I leaned in and lowered my voice, "I know you worked *really hard* on those things Des, but you are *one formal caution* away from a full dismissal. Fact is, if Ali here hadn't had the idea for the story and been willing to step up to take the flak, you'd have been on your way back to Mars now. A civilian. No more Belt cops. No more nee-nahs in space."

I sat back and hoped that would sink in.

He just laid his head on the table, groaning.

*Could have gone worse,* I thought.

Ali had remained quiet and immobile. *No sudden movements, no loud noises. She's learning.*

"Oh-khay, next on the agenda; Alison!" *Full beams on.*

"I've had a chance to go through the training manual, and what it outlines is that you'll actually only be out with us for three shifts a week, with the rest being study time here on the station."

"Yay," said a muffled Cooper.

"And one day a fortnight, you get to spend four hours on the weapons training range, practising a variety of non-lethal self-defence, both armed and unarmed."

"Really?" she said. "That sounds awesome!"

"It is," said the table, "it's the best place ever. We only get to play there once a year. This is so unfair my balls are leaving my body. Look; they're off to find somebody who has actual fun. *Be well my balls, find the happiness denied to me.*"

"Well, that's true for the most part," I said "but it says in the manual that the trainee must be accompanied and tutored by an officer with a weapons grading of five or higher. Hmm. Do we know of such an officer, Coop?"

He slowly and stiffly raised his head off the table, a packet of sugar stuck to his cheek, eyes hooded.

"I myself am an officer with a weapons grading of seven."

"Oh yes, I'd quite forgotten that! Silly old me."

Cooper's eyes moved between Ali and me, mirroring the calculations taking place in his head.

"Sooo...I get to take snotface out to the range every couple of weeks and like, play?"

"You get to take trainee Drexler out to the range and teach her the correct use of non-lethals and self-defence. This does *not* mean you get to crash glue her to a wall and fire crotch-grip at her until she wets herself, or *any* broad variation on that theme. Including Indian burns."

"Aw, come on…"

I held up the Hand of Halting.

"Ali saved your bacon yesterday, and by association mine too. As our trainee, she is also our *partner*. You are to play *nicely, professionally and safely*. Or I could get Higgs to take her, he's got weps six I think, he'll prob…"

"I'll be good."

"You promise?"

"I promise."

"Show me your hands."

"Ungh…happy?"

I checked under the table for crossed feet.

"Happy. How about it Ali, Coop's going to teach you weapons, isn't *that* nice?"

"Uh, yay?"

\*\*\*\*\*

I placed three cups of coffee and a packet of shortbread dino-shapes in front of Cooper and we left him to stew in whatever dark realm he was inhabiting.

I was still figuring out how I was going to make our new situation work, but for now, I'd drawn up a list of things to get started with. I'd put us on the dispatch board for a paperwork day before turning in the previous night. We were owed plenty, as I usually manage to keep Cooper out of harm's way by, well, doing lots of flying in deep space, with thousands of miles of hard vacuum between him and the opportunity to do harm.

Ali had tied her hair back into a ponytail of beads, and with her service-issue jumpsuit, food, sleep and hot water, already looked less like the scrawny space monkey we'd picked up on the station just yesterday. She walked beside me as we went down to the study room to fill out her first month's reading list.

"Boss?"

*Eeesh.* "Trainee Drexler?"

"Umm, look...don't think I'm not grateful and everything, 'cos I am, and I know you guys are tight, so no offence, but...letting Cooper teach me weapons....isn't that a bit...?"

"Suicidal?"

"Something along those lines, yeah."

It was a fair question, given yesterday's Cooper one-oh-one introduction course.

"I can get why you'd think that Ali, but I know Coop pretty well; we've been partners for three years, and...he's misunderstood by and large."

"Misunderstood."

"By and large."

"You screamed '...*Cooper's a fucking nutter! It'd be an unsafe educational environment!*' in front of your boss last night."

I winced. *Sigh, wince, repeat....*

"Yes, that's true. But remember what the Captain said after?"

She thought for a second.

"He's *your* nutter."

"That he is Alison, that he *is.*"

"He looks up to you."

I thought for a second.

"I guess so, but...look. Yesterday on the prowler, me and you hadn't had the best of introductions, and I'd no proof you weren't involved with those mercs, had I?"

She shook her head, beads rattling. *List: Station barber.*

"But I decided to trust you; there and then. Trust."

"So he trusts you?"

"Mnyeh, he does, but it cuts both ways. This is something you only learn on the job; *Trust your partner.*"

"But you drugged him with horse tranquiliser."

"Yes…but…"

"I said one was enough and you gave him three. You told him it was a new vitamin that lets you see through walls."

"Listen, Ali…that's not the point…what I do to…I mean *for* Cooper is always to protect him, because he's…"

"Your partner."

We stopped outside the double doors of the study room.

"Yes. My partner."

"Ok." She nodded.

"Besides," I pushed open the doors and entered the carpeted sanctum of the study room, permeated with the uncommon waft of books in space, "I know the people over on the training range, and they *definitely* know Cooper. I'll make sure they keep an eye on things," I wandered over to the bookshelves that covered the entirety of one wall and fished out the sheet of reading material I'd pulled from the training folder. I began scanning the shelves and said over my shoulder, "and seriously Ali, Coop is the highest-rated officer on the station for weapons and self-defence, it's just his thing. You'll get a few bumps and bruises on the way, but nobody is going to mess with you *whatsoever* after he's done teaching you. That boy knows 16 ways to disable an aggressor with a four-to-one weight advantage and a rotary saw using one finger - I've seen him do it."

*…after telling said hulk of a miner with a rotary saw that he'd just boffed his wife, so he could 'refine his technique under realistic field conditions'…*

I turned and saw her wide, awestruck eyes.

"Yeah. I could go for that."

"Good. Now, why the fuck do you need to read *Animal Farm*?"

## Chapter 6

I'd dropped Ali off with Lissette, the station barber, who also ran a side hustle as a minor surgeon (*for when you need confidentiality guaranteed!*) Lissete was Belt born and bred, had two young sons on a nearby FeNi station and immediately recognised Ali as one of her own. She clucked her off into her parlour to have her hair beads respectfully removed, while communing the way only true Belters could.

The mercs we'd hosed with Brown-n-down were still in the secure medical section, which posed a problem for me, as they'd not technically been arrested yet, and I needed to check they were functional enough to hear the magic words informing them of their rights, be asked if they'd understood what I'd just said, and for me to be told some variation of '*Get fucked*' in response.

The problem wasn't having a chat with the mercs - it was having to go through medical to get to them, a forced encounter with the staff who we'd forced to wade through a paddling pool of poo to get to their patients when the Krait had docked.

"Well, look who it is; Shitty McShitface, patron saint of bell-ends."

"Hi Brad. How are the perps doing?"

"Don't '*Hi Brad*' me you human cock ring. Where's Cooper the Wonder Dog? Don't think we don't know this is his work."

"Coop is feeling a little peaky today. That reminds me - peace offering."

I held out Ali's battered old backpack, her stash of '*health supplements*' from back on the station, minus the Myco23 of course. I'd already let Lissette have a rummage through, though she'd just huffed, '*What do you think I am, a vet?*'

Owen Bradley, chief medic took the bag with a suspicious slant of his eyes and tipped out the contents onto a vacant stretcher.

"Hmmn. Ooooh. Oh yeah." He looked up from the sort, "You boffing a vet or something?"

"Just recycling, doing my bit for the environment. We cool?"

"Mnurrrr....oooh, EquineSnooz 75s, they banned those..."

A couple of other medics had sensed the feeding frenzy and joined Bradley via a venomous look in my direction, so I used the distraction to wander off down the corridor to Secure Medical, the row of cells/treatment rooms where we put perps who were somewhat worse for wear on the intake to the CA justice system.

There were four of them, three men and a woman, all handily kept in one room and wearing this season's adult nappy, the must-have item for all discerning asteroid mercs. I was unsure as to how much of their encounter with Brown-n-down contributed to their ashen, skinny forms, and shuddered to think of how they'd been before the EM crew shoved several litres of fluid into their veins. They all had a variety of bandages and dressings on their heads and upper bodies, and one was in a neck brace.

I clapped my hands together once and said, "Oh-khay! My name is officer James Byron, and I'll be arresting you all today! You're being charged with the crimes of trafficking prohibited substances and bio-weapons, being in charge of an illegally armed space vessel, deep-space robbery and last but not least, interfering with Central Asset enforcement officers in their line of duty. Phew!"

They all stirred to some degree and turned their attention my way, but seemed to lack the energy to deliver the usual fuck-barrage, though I did hear an exhausted '*thrrrpsqueee*' from an orifice on my right.

"Yes, well, now that I've got your attention, I'd also like you to know that you do not have to say anything, but it may harm your defence if you do not mention when questioned something which you later rely on in court. Anything you do say may be given in evidence. So, all understood? Any questions?"

Four sets of rheumy eyes glared at me. *Tough crowd!*

I stood there for a few seconds more, then decided that the time for shakedowns, betrayals and deals would have to wait for their brains to rehydrate a bit more, and turned to leave.

*"See you at the funfair, piggie,"* croaked one of the men to my back. I turned but couldn't make out which one had spoken. *And they all had just the inkling of a smile on their pale, wrinkled lips.*

Being threatened in new and interesting ways was another standard feature of life as a Belt cop, and while this was both new and slightly creepy, it didn't stay in my mind much beyond my next encounter with Bradley on the way out.

"Perps still look pretty gnarly Brad, how long before they, you know…?"

"Stop shitting their major organs out? Worst is over, but they'll need to be on IV fluids until they stop being the human equivalent of a jet ski. Couple of days probably."

The stock of Ali's mobile drug emporium had been secreted away, her deflated backpack poking out of a waste basket. *And so turns the wheel of a working life.*

"Right, well they've been formally charged and cautioned, so they'll be going from here straight to sector 80 holding when they're fit to travel I guess; they're in no shape for interrogation right now."

"Really? Wonder why that is. Oh wait, something to do with a maniac, his handler and some shit-missile in a can?"

I gave Bradley a grade-four smile and turned to leg it out

of the medical department.

"...next time he's in here for stitching up we're going into his brain with an ice-cream scoop! Don't think we won't...."

*****

I stopped by to pick up Ali at Lissette's, complete with a utilitarian but stylish bob. She was almost a different person from yesterday, even in her demeanour. She and Lisette had obviously bonded during my duck-and-cover medical recon, and as we left, Lisette grabbed hold of me with talons that could rip a wax strip off a miner's hairy arse crack at fifty paces.

"You look after this one, treat her good. Kid's had a rough time, deserves better, you hear me? And keep that pet of yours on a short leash!"

"Come on 'Sette, you know me."

"Yeah, one man home for wayward spacers, Saint Jimbo of the cross. Humph."

*Beats 'patron Saint of bell-ends'.*

She released her grip on me with an audible click of her adamantine cherry-red fingernails.

"You need anything?" she said, instantly switching from avenging demon of justice to protective fountain of nourishment, in that way only fierce mothers can.

"Nah," I smiled, " it's all good 'Sette. Be nice if Ali can come see you now and then, while she's here on her own studying?"

Lissette furnished me with a scowl of contempt that established this had already been organised in advance, and how could I think that it wouldn't have been?

I gave her one last smile and strode off to catch up with Ali, who, like most spacers, had learned the art of discretion in small spaces at an early age.

"Lissette's really nice," she said as we wandered off to the canteen.

"Yeah, she is that," I nodded in agreement.

We walked a while in silence, Ali looking all around her at the unfamiliar sights and sounds of a working CA enforcement sector station.

We made way for a pair of cops escorting a prisoner between them, a dejected-looking miner in a blue flight jumpsuit, eyes glued to the floor. When they'd passed, Ali said, "He looked like General Transit crew, what did he do?"

I shrugged and said, "Could be anything really. Assault, smuggling, avoidance of paying child maintenance..."

As soon as I'd said the words I tensed. *Stupid, stupid...*

Although she didn't say anything I could sense a little shrinking of her good mood. *Think...*

"So, you've had dinner, breakfast, what's missing from this picture...aha, behold the glory that is a Belt cop canteen lunchtime menu!"

As I watched her finish off option three on the menu (she, wisely, going at them in numerical order to simplify matters) Cooper wandered over with a plate of his usual fish fingers, peas and mashed potato. I'd once asked him what he liked about this meal, and he'd said, "*I like the juxtaposition of straight lines, cuboids, spheres and the amorphous mass of potato.*"

What goes on in that boy's head is God's own mystery.

"Move over, snotface."

Ali did this with good grace and without breaking the stride of her food-shovelling display one iota.

"Coop."

"*James.*"

*Oh, for the love of....*

"So, I went down to medical and charged the perps from yesterday."

"Oh yeah, what kinda state they in?" *Segment the fish fingers into three, equal portions…*

I thought, and decided to steer away from any of the official medical terms Brad had used, and just said, "Tired and thirsty."

*Place a stabilising layer of mashed potato on fish finger segments…*

"Huh. Good bust eh?"

*Thank you!*

"Yep, good work all around I thought." I shared the sentiment with a glance over at Ali, who was *way* too involved with a Toad in the Hole to care. Checking back in with Coop, I found him at the *arrange the peas on top of the stabilising layer in geometric patterns* stage of his meal, his tongue stuck out a little.

I sat back and sipped my coffee.

## Chapter 7

The next few weeks went by without any major mishap, and I was genuinely surprised at how well Cooper adapted to having Ali hanging around with us, though Ali herself was responsible in large for that. Looking after herself from the age of eight, growing up on a FeNi station and being a drug dealer (though she still insisted she really *had* been a 'shamanic healer and small business entrepreneur in the health supplement sector', and me and Coop had like, *totally* taken the situation out of context) had given her personal skills way above her age, and enabled her to keep just the right distance from Coop to avoid triggering any major meltdowns while they got used to each other. Any worry about him taking her for weapons and self-defence training vanished after she returned from the first session, giddy and flushed as she limped off the shuttle.

"That was fudging *awesome!*" she gushed, and proceeded to tell me about how Coop had shown her all the best places to kick someone below the kneecap to put them down. "He like, kicked me and I'm all, 'Arrrgh!' and on the floor and shit, and then he's like, 'Now do me!' and BAM, and *he's* all like 'Arrrgh! Do it again!', and I'm..."

"Well, that sounds like fun. Did you do any weapons?"

"Oh yeah, we went on the range, with all those android people and the mock-up station? *Fudging awesome!*"

"Yes, it's good isn't it? Did Coop tell you the scoring system was broken, and hitting the people in green was the same as hitting the ones in red? Something about justice being colour blind?"

"Yes."

"Yes, I thought he may have; we'll have a chat later, but I'm glad it went well. Where *is* Coop?"

"He stayed on the station. They were showing a film called 'Watership Down'. He said it was a classic comedy or something so I didn't fancy it. Can I go see Lissette?"

"Sure, but don't bother her if she's got a client, and I want you to study the statute books later, 'kay?"

"Jawohl, mein Fuhrer!" she said, hobbling away.

"That's inappropriate, trainee Drexler," I shouted at her back.

"Yeah, Coop said you'd love it."

*Hmpf.*

\*\*\*\*\*

A few weeks later we were out on a long-planned deployment; crowd control during the 2084 Round the Belt Race, the only time in the year that there was a general homogeneity between the disparate mix of stations (other than the Belt standard hatred of us), as challenges were made, bets were taken and drinks drunk. Nearly all patrol units went out to the larger habitats 'just in case', which was without exception, always the case.

We'd pulled R92-K, a mid-tier refinery station near the middle of sector 77. The mid-tiers dealt with the asteroids that had lighter, mixed and more volatile compositions, the carbonaceous chondrites, slush and rando-rubble piles barely held together by their own gravity. Unlike the FeNi stations, there was a lot more to the average MT station and facilities technically, as there were a higher number of elements and compounds to sort out, and sometimes trans-refine before sending inwards, or out for the Belt's own use. The higher number of engineers of different sciences meant there was a deeper social stratum on MTs than the average FeNi, with the corresponding support and leisure providers. The occasional strike on a rarity-rich asteroid (especially platinum, gold and concentrations of rare earth metals) also gave MT's a particular frontier vibe, as private or small syndicate-owned prospecting ships were the primary way they found and graded their feedstock, a dumb metal detector being enough to prospect FeNi 'roids.

The early colonisers of the Belt were the large ELM (Earth, Lunar and Mars) corporations, as nobody else had the collateral for such a sphincter-ratcheting expense, but as more and more people found their way out past Mars, and once raw, refined material started to become widely available to kickstart Belt-built stations, ships to transport *more* workers and their families, small support businesses etc, the Belt started its inevitable slide to the conglomerate of smaller, independent stations, refineries, workshops and manufacturers that it is today.

The Outer Space Treaty of the 1960s prevented (in theory) any major asteroid grab, but the ELMs initially tried to tie up the entire Belt with a vast, automated AI prospecting push, which the first expansion waves of Indies were *not* happy about. So followed a whole decade of accidents, whoopsies and "I'm *sure* you said detonate" events until the ELM corporations very grudgingly sold off the bulk of their hardware and concentrated on the inner planet receiving part of the operation, which still netted them a healthy profit, if not a space empire.

People often think of the Belt as portrayed in pretty much every form of entertainment *ever,* as a dense, constantly colliding storm of asteroids, with ships slaloming around on incandescent drive flares, barely scraping by until the baddies get splatted by the world's biggest eight-ball. Such places may exist, but by and large, the Belt is a vast, empty space, and the chances of you hitting anything you're not aiming for are pretty thin. It's not that there aren't gazillions of asteroids out here, there are - it's just that there's a *lot* more space than asteroids. That's obviously boring as fuck, so a bunch of engine-heads back in the 2060's started to purposely haul some nice chunks of FeNi out of the way in the outer orbits, stuck small reaction flags on them to say "My 'roid" (little drive units that both laid legal claim to a particular rock and was capable of farting out just enough reaction to move it *verrrrry slooooowly,* which over time added up to vast distances), and made the Belt's first Round Belt race course. This is misleading, as going actually round the belt would be arse achingly long and dull, but each sector (128, count 'em) now had its own, small (by space standards) unique course, its own ship team, and once a year, eight heats of races were held in sectors right around the belt, with winners moving on towards the final, which was due to start in a couple of hours time.

We'd let Ali tag along, despite my misgivings, as she'd been bugging the *shit* out of me to come as soon as she'd heard we were deploying, and Coop thought that she could do with a 'live fire exercise'.

"But she's not allowed to carry weapons in public yet," I said, "you know that very well."

He popped his respirator on, amped up the volume and took some overly throaty breaths.

"Ah, but *she* is the weapon, and *I* am the Master…."

"We've been through this Coop, she is a CA enforcement trainee, not the pawn of an evil space entity."

"*Hufff…ah, but* **is** *she…? Hufff….*"

"Look, I'm not discussing it with you like this, nothing good ever comes of it."

"*Hufff….*"

\*\*\*\*\*

We were doing a slow, circular patrol of the main promenade, keeping a fairly low profile and neither giving nor receiving grief from the throngs of people out to watch the final race in the station's bars, cafes and social spaces. There were a decent number of families out, and as far as Belt deployments went, this rated quite high in terms of wholesome and safe, and low in Coop's rating of exciting and violent, though the night was young and the Belt was the Belt, always.

"So, what do we do if we see a fight?" Ali asked me, all eyes and ears for her surroundings.

"First thing is just to make our presence known really," I said, looking down over the railing to the lower level "same as we're doing now. Sometimes that's all you need to do to calm things down, demonstrate you can terminate their fun. You know as well as anyone how hard most Belters work; they just want to have fun by and large. Our main weapon is being able to take that away from them."

"Speak for yourself," said Coop, fingers brushing over his collection of non-lethals, admittedly well vetted by me every morning to make sure he was only packing standard issue heat, and not the can of actual 'Heat' I'd caught him with last week.

*"This is for culinary use, you're always saying I need to vary my meals more!"* - *"I meant have a few more greens and fruit, not medium rare leg of miner!"*

"And what if that doesn't break up the fight? What if they start to fight with us?" Ali continued.

"Ah, that is when you extinguish your tofu-scented candles and become a real cop, not..." he flicked his fingers at me, "...*this*. The time for violence will be at hand."

Ali looked from Coop to me.

"I've never denied that a Belt cop sometimes needs to use

force to police an unruly situation, Ali, merely that it should always be the final resort, *not*," I looked over her head at Coop, "the default option."

"Pffft, you show me one single place in the rules where it says that," said Coop, a sudden roar of drunken cheering off to his right capturing his attention.

"It's literally on our badges. One of which you're wearing; *Protect, cherish and serve.*"

"Marketing. Doesn't count."

He was heading towards a knot of refinery workers playing some sort of drinking game, and I hurried to catch up and mitigate any...*unpleasantries.*

*****

Despite his best efforts, and with me running interference, Coop couldn't fabricate any sort of encounter with the refiners or any other rowdy bunches, and had stopped trying, now just stalking along quietly by Ali and me. Sometimes Coop just went into quiescent mode, off in his own frightening realms.

The race had just started, and much of the crowd's attention was on the action, the insanely overpowered ships slewing around the course pulling G forces that would put a normal passenger in a hospital or morgue. There were very few restrictions on what you could build, and devices for coping with the Gs were as big a part of the design of race entrants as the ships and engines, and about as dangerous. Machinery for forcing blood from one part of the body to another, or preventing it (and the resulting blackouts, aneurysms etc) was a recipe for disaster, and failures were often fatal. There were sometimes calls for tighter regulations, if particularly gruesome incidents left a pilot resembling a half-eaten calzone dropped in a bowl of salsa, for example, but the Belt (being the Belt) soon shouted them down as being nanny state micromanagement.

We'd perched ourselves on some public seating for a break and were getting into some doughnut balls and Frutee Fizz with a decent view of a screen outside a coffee shop. As one we contracted inward with an *'Ooooh!'* as sector 35's racer lost control flipping around a marker, his main flare open a fraction of a second out of synch with his nose jet as he flipped, clipping said nose into the 'roid and causing an instant spin that blurred the ship into a disc. That was the kind of crash that could flatten the pilot with rotational Gs, sometimes taking hours or days for the rescue crew to snag it back under control.

"Spam in a can," said Coop, licking sugar crystals off his fingers.

"Way it goes," I concurred, nodding.

Ali was *way* too involved with her food to join in with the time-honoured sports *'yup'* expected of her.

"Attention Belters! Attention Belters!"

The audio was harsh and clipped, recorded for volume and not subtlety. *And coming from the TVs…who was this woman on the screen?*

"My name is Kavine LaVelle, leader of the Free Belt Army. We apologise for interrupting the final race of the season, but we have a message for you that could not wait."

The clamour of the station had died down to a murmur, Coop was frozen with a finger in his mouth and I started to get a cold feeling down my back. *Free Belt Army?*

"Since the dawn of the Belt, when we humans first became settlers, and then Belters, there has always been a stain left on our brave new country in the stars, a bitter taste left of the planets we left and outgrew. As we became the people that we are today, masters of these spacelands, we carried along a parasite of the old world, clinging and sucking at our freedoms. Sure, we still trade with Earth, the Moon and Mars; we have what they want, and they have some things we want. That's just trade. That's fair.

"But do you know what's *not* fair? What we *don't* want and yet they give it to us anyway? *Their laws! Their laws and the pigs who stuff them down our throats!*"

Among the general murmur came the unmistakable noises of agreement, *yeahs, mmmns,* and also the quiet sound of safety caps being popped across the table.

"Ali?" I said, quietly.

"Uh-huh," she said, swallowing her catering-sized doughnut with some difficulty.

"We're going to slowly walk back towards the docks, and I want you to stay close and quiet."

She just nodded.

Coop stood up and as he came round the table I saw him slide a slim green cylinder into Ali's pocket, tapping her hip to draw attention to it. The orange top showed it was ready for use, Vom-stopper. Coop was calmly gazing along the promenade, so she looked at me.

"Red robots only, ok?"

She gave me a nervous smile.

I corralled her in between us with Coop on point and we sauntered off spinward. It wasn't far to the docks and the waiting prowler, but it was far enough to get in a world of trouble. *What was this LaVelle woman trying to do?*

Her voice followed us as we walked, sticking close to the promenade railings, the crowd thankfully still mostly looking inward at the video screens in the bars and shops, though the occasional look came our way.

"We of the Free Belt Army have been working for your freedom for years, though you will not have heard or seen our efforts. For years we have been quietly planning, arming and preparing the Belt for this day, for this day of FREEDOM!"

This time there wasn't a general rise in agreement, there were real roars of approval, no doubt helped by the drinking festivities of....

'*See you at the funfair, piggie....*'

"Mother*fudgers!*"

# Chapter 8

Coop and Ali's heads snapped back to look at me. I mouthed "*Sorry*" at them and ushered them forward.

The atmosphere was turning decidedly ugly, and while we Belt cops were perfectly used to being 'the enemy' among crowds, it was suddenly rather different to be '*The Enemy*'.

While Coop is, in heart and soul, a go-for-the-jugular predator, he's not stupid. Doubtless, if he'd had another can of Brown-n-down it'd already have been tossed into the central atrium and he'd be taking pictures for his cherished moments album, but in the situation we were in, he knew that the closer we were to the prowler the better combat odds we had. It's hard for people not to draw conclusions about Coop when he's full-on banzai, but they're getting the wrong impression if they think that's *all* he is.

"An hour ago, attacks were launched on *every* CA enforcement sector station in the belt, and I am proud to tell you that as of now, every station is under the control of the Free Belt Army! Belt laws for Belters!"

Now the uproar was joined by smashing sounds, as chairs were flung around, tables overturned and glasses started flying everywhere.

We were in sight of the broad cut through to the docks when the first challenge came, in the form of a flying potted plant that detonated just in front of Coop, spraying all of us with soil.

There were about ten roughnecks, with a less committed backing group around double the size behind them.

"Come on then, fucking pigs! Think you're hard?"

I held my empty hands out and slowly walked towards them.

"All right lads, calm down, I don't know what this…"

Coop stepped out from behind me, having used me to get within range and opened up with a can of crotch-gripper.

The effect of the electrically boosted and ion-delivered crotch-gripper is widely described as being kicked in the balls, giving birth, having the opposite of an orgasm, or all three at once. As one, the group of 'necks fell to their knees in gonad-clenching agony. A squeal behind me made me whip around. Two of their mates had snuck around and were closing on us from either side, close to the promenade railings. As one ran towards Ali she raised her can of vomstop and gave him a short but well-aimed burst right in the face at about ten feet. The effect, like crotch-grip, was almost instant, and in the space of a heartbeat, every muscle in his body was retasked to removing the contents of his stomach. Ali squealed again and flattened herself against the railings as a solid beam of spew flashed past her. Then my attacker was on me, broken bottle in hand. He jabbed at my face, once, twice, then went for a wide slash at my neck. As his arm was off to the side, I drew an arc at his unprotected neck myself, the telescoping shockstick in my hand extending and delivering 10kv of juice straight into his nervous system, along with a crisp smack. He collapsed like a dropped bag of shopping. I quickly looked around to check how things stood.

Ali's mark was convulsively heaving on the floor, dribbling green bile and making vomit angels in the mess, and Coop was still intermittently hosing the original group of 'necks, their howls of pain acting as a deterrent to the rest of the observers, milling angrily and hooting obscenities but staying well out of range.

"Oh-khay I think we've made our point here, shall we meander?"

Coop gave a grunt and hosed one last burst of crotch-grip at the whimpering tangle of bodies. We walked away slowly, me waving Ali closer to us, keeping an eye over our shoulders but not backing away, and certainly not running. *Show no fear.*

The docks were almost deserted but for some confused workers who knew something was afoot but not the details. The sight of the prowler on its docking pylon was sweet and the closing of the hatch behind us was a relief.

"Is it true, what she said about the attacks on the sector stations?" asked Ali, as we strapped ourselves in and prepped the ship. I exchanged a look with Coop and pulled up the CA dispatch board on the console.

"Nothing from home," I said, scrolling around the adjacent sectors to the 77th, then pausing on the 85th. "Shit. 85th got an APB out about forty-five minutes back. *Under attack from several armed merc ships, narco gas harpoons, many down, mercs attempting to dock, send help.*"

I looked up. Ali was white, Coop thoughtful.

"All the stations would be pretty much empty other than support staff, prisoners, the brass…we're all out here policing the final," I said, piecing together the bigger picture.

"Good plan," said Coop, appreciatively. "If they got all, or even some of the stations, that's a whole lot of bases, hardware and hostages."

"And the patrols out here, right in the middle of it all. We were lucky to get out."

"Fuck luck, superior firepower is the only game in town. Nice hit with the vom-stopper, snotface," said Coop setting up for a manual disengagement. We'd no way of knowing who was in control of dock approach, and it was prudent that we got out of Dodge quickly, without finesse or comms to a possibly hostile control room.

"Uh, yeah. Thanks for, like…"

"*CA vessel on pylon 32C, you are not cleared for departure. This station is now under the control of the FBA and you are under arrest.*

*Prepare for boarding."*

"How we doing Coop?" I asked, losing track of what he was doing on the console and wisely staying out of his way.

"Not far."

"R92K dock approach, this is CA enforcement vessel 77-14 Scamp. Please be aware that we are declaring a class five bio lockdown aboard this vessel due to a contagious outbreak, please do not enter. Over."

*"CA vessel, don't try that with us, prepare to be boarded and know that resistance will be met with lethal force."*

"R92K dock approach, this is CA enforcement vessel 77-14 Scamp. No, seriously, we are carrying miners infected with severe venereal pustule syndrome, if you don't believe me please open a video link to our holding bay; sending you the invite."

*"Don't be stupid, if you thin…what…ERRRRGH!"*

What I *did* send was a link to a WhamstaGram video from #WorstSpotSqueezEva that Coop had forwarded *me* a few weeks back under the auspices of researching 'offensive psychological weaponry'. Some poor soul with a pustule the size of a grapefruit giving it the heave-ho and it ending up all over the camera lens. It was actually pretty effective, as Coop had timed me having an *eeewww!* convulsion for around four seconds, which any fighter will tell you is a big advantage in a scrap.

"Nice one Jimbo," he said, fist bumping me over the centre console, "aaaand, we're out of here."

I heard the rapid staccato of a manual clamp disengage rattle through the hull, and Coop smoothly pirouetted the prowler round towards the dock doors. Which were closing, obviously.

"Are we going to maKEEEE!"

Coop simply engaged full thrust, and if we scraped by or passed with a decent, if less cinematic margin, I've no idea, as the G-force pushed my eyeballs back into their sockets and my vision narrowed to a blurry patch dead ahead. Just as violently the drive shut off and all our jelly bits sprang forward into a new chapter of discomfort.

"Yerrg, CoOOO!"

In less than a second, Coop had vectored us *somewhere* and hit maximum burn again, and my vision once more narrowed, and narrowed, and nar....

## Chapter 9

"....wuurrgh," I said.

"Foof," replied Coop.

"Nnnng...urrrh," agreed Ali.

We all sat there for a while, recovering from whatever Gs we'd pulled for however long. Sometimes the universe can just fuck off, whether you're headed into a black hole or not.

"Well, that was interesting," I finally ventured. It felt like my jaw had been dislocated. I turned my head to check on Ali behind us and really wished I hadn't. "Eeeeng. Ali?"

"Are we dead? If not, can we be, please? I think my pelvis is back on the station."

"Probably best to move forward with what you've got left. Nice flying Coop, or did we just explode in a general direction?"

"Skills and thrills all the warrrrhg!"

A very audible crunch-pop came from Coop's shoulder as he raised his arm to the console, which made me and Ali both wince, which also *really fucking hurt.*

"Nnnng, 'sok, gone back in," he hissed through gritted teeth.

"Fuck me," I said, and we all sat there for another few minutes, oblivious of anything other than our creaking joints and oozing organs.

"Where are we?" I finally asked.

"Heading out, roughly towards the trojans, I didn't do much more than point us away from the station on a timed burn."

I was confused for a moment, as we'd been heading away before he made that course change, then realised he meant *our* station, not R92K. I thought for a few seconds about this. There was a really good chance this LaVelle woman was telling the truth, and that if we'd headed back to 'help', we'd have been heading back to an occupied CA enforcement station guarded by armed mercs who'd already killed god knows how many of our fellow cops already. I looked at Coop and saw more than physical pain on his face.

"Hey, buddy - you made exactly the right call, we'll fight another day, ok? I mean it."

He relaxed a microscopic amount, but I knew he'd reacted against a whole herd of velociraptor bloodlust, and that he'd have to have whatever fucked up internal pow-wow among his spirit animals to sort it out, so I moved on.

"Anyone fancy a cup of tea?"

For some reason, this was the funniest thing anyone had said on a spaceship, *ever*, and we all located several cracked ribs laughing ourselves stupid.

"I'll put the kettle on," said Ali, wiping tears off her face and tentatively unstrapping her seat harness.

As she limped into the galley alcove I took stock of our course on the nav console. As Coop had said, we were heading out at a pretty good clip towards the trojans, the clump of asteroids out of the main Belt that shares the same orbit as Jupiter at Lagrange point four. The main industrial activities and the bulk of Belter presence were further inward towards the sun, where delta-V was cheaper and facilities closer together. Again I marvelled at Coop's split-second decision to escape outwards, rather than the familiar inner sector we knew so well. There certainly were Belters out here, prospectors mainly, but there were also some habitats ranging from a few hundred souls to lone crazies, gone mad contemplating the void. Belters out here were different, and decidedly stranger than the inner and mid Belters, less involved with commerce between ELM and each other. Maybe the mood out here would be different too, and we could find a safe harbour?

A prowler never leaves the service bay without a full tank of reaction fuel, emergency food rations for ten days and backup air and water purifiers should the main ones give up. We were ok for now, but we couldn't go on for long. Mars was totally out of the question, even if we'd started a course from the station, and I had as much burning hatred to fight back against these free fucking Belt arseholes as Coop. Ok, maybe not as much as Coop; he probably had that level of burning hatred when he didn't get a toy in his morning bowl of Krispy Loopz.

I took a fuel reading and pulled up our options on the charts. We were running dark, ID transponder off. There were no ships in ID range, but we couldn't risk firing up our own (now boring) scanner, which would announce our presence to all. I quickly checked our log, and it told of no active sweeps since leaving the station, so it seemed like we were in the clear, though we couldn't totally discount pursuers. Within our deceleration cone there were very few highlighted destinations. Some were without information at all, and could be anything from a lone hermit (possibly deceased) in a single-seat ship, glommed onto a 'roid, to uninhabited utilities or abandoned workings - habitats that were started but never finished through a calamity or richer pickings found elsewhere. There were a handful of widely scattered, small logistic hubs servicing prospectors and the locale, but they were likely to be inner Belt aligned. In the end, the choice was made for us; Gracelands, population one hundred and eighty-three, religious retreat, privately funded.

*Sounds harmless enough.*

\*\*\*\*\*

Flight time to Gracelands was around three days, so we had time to recover somewhat from our high-G injuries, and we dug out an unofficial stash of decent painkillers we'd liberated some months back. For the first forty-eight hours we all slept in shifts, one person always on the watch for pursuers. There was the occasional blip of an anti-collision scan flailing around, probably from prospectors, but nothing to cause undue worry. Not that we much cared in the pillowy warmth of OuchEaze max strength. Two days in and we were in much better shape.

We'd been listening to the Belt-wide radio network to get more information on what had taken place and what was happening. It was impossible to know for sure how much was propaganda, but it appeared that the Belt government had pretty much said '*Meh, whatever*' to the takeover of the Belt cops by the FBA. This was actually fairly believable, as the 'government' out here is such a nebulous and barely visible construct that some people think it's largely an urban myth, with the motto '*If they can't count you, you're not accountable!*' widely quoted.

There was no news on the fate of our compadres, or any sector station-based staff, just that all former CA enforcement stations were now 'under FBA control'. We knew that the majority of patrols had been out on stations, and had probably run into the same kind of trouble we had, but had no way of contacting them without broadcasting our presence via data relay stations. For now, we were on our own.

"Do we know anything about this Gracelands place?" asked Ali, fishing for the last crumbs in a bag of Star Gems.

"Just what it said on the chart, privately funded religious retreat, couple of hundred people give or take. No way of knowing more without hooking up to the net."

"There was a girl on my station from out here, escaped stowed away in an automated shipment of volatiles. Lost some toes and fingers to frostbite on the way."

"Escaped from what?" I asked, automatically cradling my fingers around my warm mug of tea.

"Some religious nutjob place her family moved to, something to do with radio waves from God?"

I thought for a moment, "Receivers of the Word?"

"Thassit. You know about them?"

"Mmmn, not much. They come out here and move to the outer edges of the belt, spend hours and hours every day in tethered suits, supposedly listening for transmissions from the big fella. The thing is, that's pretty much like floating in a sensory deprivation tank and they're actually hallucinating like, oooh, I dunno…they were dosed with a mycotoxin that…"

"Aw, c'mon man, you ever going to let that go?" she groaned.

I just smiled at her.

"So your pal from the outer limits, what happened to her?"

Ali withdrew into herself a little and said, "Nothing good."

"Ah."

In the few weeks we'd known her, Ali had come on so much from the person we'd found that I'd forgotten what a grindingly bleak existence she'd come up through.

"Well, I've heard nothing about this place good or bad on the grapevine," I said, "probably a good sign. Lots of people out here just want peace and quiet."

"We should treat them as hostile, pump narco gas in," yawned Coop, surfacing from a snooze.

"That's your solution to everything," said Ali.

*Aw.*

\*\*\*\*\*

We announced our presence forty minutes out from docking

on the short-range radio, the first active emission we'd made in days. I pruned the official approach call, not knowing what reaction we'd get to announcing an inbound CA enforcement vessel. They'd make us soon enough, but we stood to gain more by docking than getting locked out. We were running low on fuel, food and most crucial of all, teabags.

"Gracelands approach, this is 77-14 Scamp requesting an expedited dock please, we ran into a little trouble and could use some help."

After a longer-than-usual pause, we got a response.

"Heyyyy! Scampi and fries! Come on in, the water's fine!"

"Rather formal," I said.

"Definitely hostile," growled Coop.

"Oh-khay, I have control this time officer Cooper, taking us in."

"Mind the fuelling pylon. James. MIND THE, oh for fu…"

"*Really* not helping."

"Is he allowed to fly this?" asked Ali.

"Hmmf. Allegedly."

"Shut up, both of you. There."

The prowler shuddered violently as the docking clamps made the adjustment for my perfectly adequate docking angle.

Coop just looked at me.

"Piss off, Maverick."

"Are they throwing us a welcoming party?" asked Ali.

"Well, they sounded nice enough on the radio."

"No, look," she said, pointing through the flight deck window.

Besides it being a riot of coloured shapes, I didn't quite understand the sight that was approaching down the pylon walkway for a few seconds, then suddenly, I did.

"Huh. You don't see that too often."

It was indeed a welcoming party. Some twenty or so belters in Hawaiian shirts, tie-dyed shorts and dresses were closing in, bearing garlands of flowers and trays of what looked like finger food and pineapples sprouting straws.

Coop was making a high, keening noise.

"It's ok, nothing to be scared of, they're just being friendly," I said in a singsong to him. This was *way* out of his comfort zone.

"Right, here's the plan, be careful accepting any…"

Ali barreled into the crowd outside and seemed to have developed three extra pairs of hands in order to efficiently cram stuffed vine leaves, sausage rolls and pina colada into her face, much to the approval of our hosts who proceeded to cheer her on and garnish her with flowers.

"Has that girl got tapeworms?" I asked.

# Chapter 10

It took me a few minutes to prise Coop out of his catatonic paralysis and persuade him that the welcoming committee were just 'being nice', like the clowns had been when I took him for a birthday meal at Face Burger last year.

"Look, they've got a tray of muffins. You *love* muffins!"

"What flavour are they?" he asked suspiciously.

"Chocolate, blueberry…sardine, how do…"

I gathered myself.

"I'm sure they've got whatever flavour you want."

"Mnnnehhh…."

"Right, off we go then. Behave."

As we stepped out of the main hatch a large, rotund man with grey frizzy hair turned to greet us.

"Heyyy! Better late than never, welcome to Gracelands dudes!"

He came forward and gave me a big hug, enveloping me in a solid waft of coconut, weed, and rum.

"Errr, yes. Thank you!"

He broke off and turned to Coop with an enormous smile. Coop looked like he was about to run away screaming, so I put a hand on the big man's pudgy arm and said, "My friend is recovering from a traumatic experience involving a vat full of cloned limbs, and he's *really* pleased to meet you but is a little squeamish about hugs right now?"

"Aw, really? That sucks so *much!*"

"I know. He's normally such a touchy-feely sort of guy too. I'm James, and this is Desmond, call us Jim and Des, please."

"Heyyy! My new friends Jim and Des! Everybody, it's Jim and Des!"

""Heyyy Jim and Des, aloha!" came the chorused welcome. Coop looked like he'd just had a liquid nitrogen enema.

"And the walking digestive system over there you've met already, Ali."

"Yeah, we love Ali, girl can *eat!* Harrrr!"

"Yes, we've noticed that too."

Ali gave me a happy wave that perfectly utilised the motion to also transfer a samosa past her doubled daiquiri delivery tubes.

"So, you guys said you'd had a little trouble?"

"Ah, yes. Been watching the news much?"

"Not really, but we heard what happened. Bummer."

"Yes. Aaand, we being…you know…"

"Cops?"

"Yes."

"Pffft, you never gave us any bother. In fact, you came out and warned off some GrindCorp dudes who were harshing our mellow a few years back. Bunch of prospectors claimed we were sitting on a big wodge of platinum and '*not utilising resources in a Belt-like manner*'. Not cool man, not cool."

"Really? Well, we're glad we could help you out. Look, to be honest, we're really in a bit of a pickle and we're not sure what our plan is yet, but we wondered if…"

"Heyyy, say no more man - you dudes can crash here as long as you need, take a load off and recalculate your karmic calendar, yeah?"

"I'm not entirely sure of what you just offered, but I think that would be really kind of you regardless, thank you."

I looked over to the prowler, grimy and battered but very much a big old space nee-nah.

"Have you got anywhere we could hide our ship? I'd hate to bring any trouble down on you if you get a visit from the inners."

"Heyyy, Kevin! What's in cargo bay three?"

"It's empty boss," shouted a long-haired boy around Ali's age, tuning up a guitar.

"Nil problemo guys, I'm sure we can fit your wheels somewhere!" he said, giving us yet another massive gold-toothed smile.

"That's really great, thanks…err, we didn't catch your name?"

"Elvis. Elvis Presley, at your service boys!"

"Yes. Well, so pleased to meet you, Elvis. Big fan."

Coop looked like he'd moved on to anal liquid hydrogen, and Ali looked like she couldn't decide whether to eat Kevin or another halloumi kebab.

\*\*\*\*\*

In a nice change to our luck, Elvis and his entourage turned out to be no weirder than the Belt median, and certainly a lot less angry. Their 'religion' was mostly based on 'being cool and having a good time'. Cooper was initially terrified, then bored witless.

"What's your boy's thing, Jim? He's unhappy and that's not cool," asked the Big Kahuna one day as I cleaned out the prowler's reaction premix chamber in the station workshop. We'd decided to sit tight, watch and wait for a few weeks, either to let things cool off, see if ELM sent some kind of force in, or get some idea of how we could escape to Mars. Ali had said, "We could just stay here, Elvis said it'd be really cool and we'd be welcome." I said it was an option and left it at that. And did not start singing "Ali and Kevin, sitting in a tree…", at all.

"Cooper's…difficult to please," I said to Elvis, searching for something to get the carbon out of a swirling groove.

"Heyyy, surely there's something we can do for him? What's he into?"

"Intense danger and physical violence," I laughed, "You

guys are way too cool for that - in the nicest possible way," I added.

"I dig that, but we aim to please man, we aim to please. Has he met Layla yet?"

"Layla?"

"Yeah. She's something else, really into the Eastern arts. They'd have a lot in common I think."

I doubted that very much but said it was worth a go.

It turned out that 'Eastern arts' included several styles of kung fu, and Cooper's initial 'whatever' rebuff to her greeting led to him getting kicked in the balls, punched in the throat, and headbutted in the nose so hard we were worried bone splinters had penetrated his brain.

They were pretty much inseparable after that, and I was thinking a fall wedding would suit them best. Coop is definitely an Autumn.

"Always the bridesmaid," I said wistfully one day, as I watched Coop showing Layla his favourite Aikido wrist locks and Ali showing Kevin the correct method of eating a triple fried-egg sandwich while retaining optimum yolk distribution.

Gracelands had a truly beautiful landscaped central atrium, where 'The Cool' as they called themselves came every day to play frisbee, eat, drink, smoke weed and generally not have a care in the world. I had a nice spot where I'd taken to sitting listening to BR4 on my personal radio linked to the prowler, hoping to get some news pertinent to our situation. There had been very little to go on really, the Belt and ELM seemingly having shrugged off the whole affair and going on about its business. This had left me pretty angry, all told. The Belt cops hadn't been perfect, but we'd laid our lives on the line plenty of times, and for what? For the whole solar system to say *'Meh, we didn't like them anyway.'* Bastards.

I was in one of these moods when I noticed the signal on

the radio dropping in and out, and some hint at another transmission vying for attention. *That's the long-range set!*

I'd left the prowler's long-range encrypted set open on the calling channel; it was supposed to override anything else while receiving a transmission but the squelch must have been too wide, and the commercial transmission kept popping back up. *Shit!*

"Today, member stati..ops, rall..ened to disc..den, rally po..ding bilateral tra..belt cops, ra…ment with ELM, wit..oint eden, r..opes of increasing levels of volatiles in the future. In other news…."

*Belt cops. Rally. Oint? Eden? Ointment? Point Eden? Rally point Eden? Where had I heard that before?*

I thought about how this was being broadcasted. The transmission itself was encrypted and could selectively allow prowler-only decryption, blocking any station equipment from hearing the message, but it was on a Belt-cop-only frequency, so the FBA would know *something* was being transmitted, and the source could be traced by triangulating the relay stations. Then I imagined a prowler, set to repeat the broadcast and sent off on an autopilot max burn orbit of the belt, the deceleration fuel burned as well. Not an easy thing to catch going at those speeds - it'd also explain the fleeting nature of the transmission. So long as the FBA hadn't captured any prowlers, complete with live cops to unlock the biometrics (tech long having got over the literal hack of severing a hand to use fingerprints, now using scanned faces 'not under duress' in order to turn the ignition key, and would lock out systems after repeated failed attempts), there was a good chance that this message was secure, and only cops on the run could hear it.

I wandered over to Coop and Layla.
"Hey Layla, nice reverse headlock!"

"Heyyy, Jimbo, thanks baby!" she smiled at me expansively, simultaneously torquing Coop's head backwards and applying pressure to a straight arm lock, "these wrist locks work just *great* with it!"

"Yes, Coop looks like he's in *tremendous* pain. Hey Coop!"

"Gaaak, nnng, 'imbo. 'Sup?"

"Oh, nothing much. Can we have a chat?"

Coop reached up to tap out a submission on Layla's arm, and she immediately dropped him on his back and shook herself out.

I gave him a few seconds to reconnect his vertebrae.

"Listen, I just heard a transmission on the long-range encrypted set, but it was garbled. *'Belt cops, rally point Eden'*, just that, repeated."

"Huh. That sounds familiar," he said.

"It does, but I still haven't a clue."

"Clue about what?" asked Ali, sauntering over.

"Rally point Eden."

"Huh. That sounds familiar."

"I just said that," said Coop.

"Yes, alright, we've established we're three fuckwits who don't know what 'Rally point Eden' means, but think we actually do. Can we maybe pool our meagre brain capacities to figuring out…"

"Did you say rally point Eden?" asked Layla.

"Nnnng. Yes, Layla. We did."

"Pretty deserted these days, long trip now the mine's worked out, no shuttles to hitch onto. Used to go there racing monopods with my brothers."

The Three Fuckwits gazed at the small, perfectly muscled form of Layla, stretching her deltoids, punching Cooper for the use of.

"So, you know where this place is?" I asked, stupidly.

"Course I do! Out in sector 23, outer edge. *Wayyy* out."

The Fuckwit Three stared at her some more.

"The original racetrack? The one the engine heads built before they constructed the new ones, closer in? There's a worked-out platinum mine there called Point Eden."

"Belt cops, rally at Point Eden," I said, looking at Coop and Ali.

*We're still in the game!*

## Chapter 11

Despite our best efforts over the next couple of days, we didn't hear anything else on the long-range set, even when we risked taking the prowler out into deep space to get a better signal.

"Could be a trap," said Coop, not for the first time, as he took us back into the dock at Gracelands. The thing was, this wasn't his usual paranoid assumption of ever-present hostile intentions, like the time we had Christmas carol singers arrive at the sector station and he barricaded himself in his room. This time, he was right.

I blew my cheeks out in exasperation. "Yeah. Tricky one."

This wasn't the only thing giving us pause for thought. In the time spent at Gracelands, both Coop and Ali had grown attached to Layla and Kevin respectively, and we'd all relaxed into the friendliness and acceptance of the place and its people, which for Cooper was a minor miracle, though he was mostly orbiting around Layla and her vivacious violence. Combined with the overall impression that the Belt couldn't care less about the passing of the Belt cops, we were all lukewarm at best about the idea of risking our lives by flying off to Point Eden and some notional fightback by the Belt cops. Fight back to what, the Belt saying '*Whatever*'? Fuck that.

Ali, understandably, was less bothered, but me and Coop were pretty sullen. We'd been cops for years, and there was something instilled in us after looking out for each other, as partners and as part of the larger force, and we couldn't let it go that easily. But still, we made no decision to move either.

Then Gracelands had a visit from the FBA, which helped clarify matters somewhat.

*****

"Boss, we got incoming attitudes, 'bout forty minutes away. Said they were FBA and we were to let them dock. Didn't say please."

I sat up quickly from my sun lounger, Ali taking a step back and fidgeting nervously.

"You seen Coop, Elvis?"

"They're in the control room, sent me to find you."

"Right. Let's see what we can do about it then," I said airily, not wanting to add to her nervousness.

As we walked towards the entrance of the service levels I tried to formulate our options.

"Listen, if the mercs find us, they're probably only looking for me and Coop - I can't imagine they'd consider we'd have a trainee your age with us, so if we're caught, you stay quiet, ok?"

She looked at me in a way that didn't signal she was happy about this.

"Ali, look at me." I pulled her up and turned to face her.

"This is not your fight, and these people don't play by our rules. Me and Coop are both really proud of you, but you signed on for being a Belt cop trainee, not....whatever we are now, so you *stay quiet, ok?*"

She looked at me with a mixture of defiance, ridicule and contempt that only a teenager can properly pull off.

"You're both *really proud* of me?"

"Look, this isn't the time..."

"Like, you're my *adoptive parents* and Coop is your *life partner?*"

"Not listening! Lalala..." I said, walking away with my fingers in my ears.

"...but you won't get to see me go to the prom, or..."

I started running and arrived at the control room out of breath.

"That girl," I said, panting and pointing to the door, "does *not* get her bad attitude from *me*, Desmond Cooper, do you hear me?"

He did, and to his credit, let the matter slide to focus on the incoming space bastards.

"Got a positive ID on them," he said, "it's a GN class freighter, 'Bobblehead'. Even if they've not tooled up, it's got minibeams."

As large ships (or ones towing large asteroidal masses, as some did) lacked the manoeuvrability of smaller vessels, they often came fitted with lasers capable of vaporising objects up to the size of an apple, which was a much easier collision avoidance method than vectoring thousands of tonnes of ship out of the way, and then back on course. While other ships/stations were a lot bigger than an apple, searing a fruit-sized hole through them was still fairly effective in de-peopling terms. There were a lot of safety systems built in to prevent them from being used this way, but it wasn't rocket surgery to simply disconnect everything barring the power supply to the lasing tube and aim it using the ship itself and an on-off switch to the power.

I looked at Coop, who as usual showed little concern, though a glint at conflict afoot was in his eye. Ali smirked into the room but read the mood and stood down.

"Options," I said, "we make a run for it, but there's no chance we'd not be seen, and we don't know how they'd treat everyone here for harbouring us, *but,* if you want us off the station, Elvis, we'll go anyway, and we're truly sorry for any blowback."

Elvis stayed quiet, but had a thoughtful look on his face, as he considered the wellbeing of his flock.

"Option two, and again I'm sorry to put you in this

position, but if you allow it, we'll try and hide, wait for them to leave, and *then* get out of town. This isn't fair on you, we already owe you so much, and it's time we moved on."

He nodded, relaxed his pose and said, "Heyy, don't sweat it man, we all love you, you know that. If you want to stay, you stay, go, you go, we'll be fine here. The Cool shall prevail, always."

He graced us all with a smile that conveyed true faith in the power of coolness. This was kinder than he knew, as what I hadn't voiced was the fact that even if Coop kept us out of the crosshairs of weaponry and got up to a speed the larger ship couldn't match, we'd have very little choice in where we were heading, and had stupidly not made preparations for such a hasty exit. We'd all moved our eyes off the ball in this relaxing place, and now we were paying for it.

I looked at Coop and nodded minutely. He knew our position as well as I did.

"Right. The prowler…"

Elvis, seeming to know our decision said, "We've got a whole pod full of pineapple-shaped ukuleles that got sent up in error a few years back; we can pack them into cargo bay three to hide it."

"That would work," I smiled at our grey, frizzy friend who had appeared when we needed one most.

"Automatic baby, KEVIN!..." he bellowed, and departed to organise the prowler's Hawaiian camouflage scheme. Then I considered our own.

"We need some new clothes," I said, looking at the three of us. While we'd divested ourselves of our tactical harnesses, belts and hats (though I did see Coop sneaking out of Layla's yurt in full combat attire the other morning), we were still wearing enough uniform to be made as cops.

"We should go down to the gardens, ask some of The Cool," said Ali.

So we did.

## Chapter 12

"That looks really good on you Coop. You're definitely an Autumn," said Ali, as she took stock of his muted earth tone outfit, lots of flowing, naturally dyed cotton, "that turmeric batik work really matches your eyes."

"Is she taking the piss?"

"She may be, but she's also not wrong," I said appreciatively.

He whined a little and sagged into quiescent mode.

I myself had gone for the de-rigueur migraine-inducing Hawaiian shirt and cut-off jeans common among The Cool, Ali opting for a ragged surf t-shirt and shorts. We all had face-obscuring hats we could slouch under, and were as ready as we'd ever be to meet the mercs. We'd decided the best plan would be to hide in plain sight among The Cool. We'd no idea if they were looking for us or just paying a social visit, but we were about to find out.

The freighter docked onto the sole cargo pylon capable of clamping a ship of that size, and Elvis and Kevin led a small welcoming party, this time sans buffet and garlands. We hung well back and close to the dock doors but wanted to be near enough to see and hear what was happening, keep on top of whatever situation transpired.

Six mercs clumped down the ramp onto the walkway, all wearing heavy combat boots, a *lot* of black leather, and every one of them was armed with either a rifle or holstered gun, along with vests full of other offensives.

I felt Coop tense beside me and quietly said, "Be cool, everything's cool," despite feeling the situation was anything but.

"Heyyy! Welcome to Graceland dudes, happiest station in the outer belt!" said Elvis, arms wide in welcome.

*Don't hug him!*

He didn't.

"Who's in charge here?" snapped the foremost of the mercs, a bald, sneering hulk of a man in a leather waistcoat, bulging bare arms and bandoliers of projectile ammunition everywhere he could fit one. Considering he had a beam pistol on his hip, this was just macho jewellery. There's utilitarianism and then there's bondage apparel. He looked past Elvis at the gathered Cool with unconcealed scorn.

"That'll be me, Elvis P at your service," he beamed.

The rest of the mercs looked at each other and exchanged some snorts of entertainment.

"Yeah, well, see Mr Elvis, as representatives of the Free Belt Army, we've been tasked with collecting overdue taxes owing to the Belt government, such as it is, and we've been informed that due to the high platinum content of this 'roid, you've been re-assessed, backdated and now owe somewhere in the region of 200kg of refined platinum."

"200kg," said Elvis, flatly.

"Somewhere in the region of."

Elvis held his gaze for a few seconds, though I couldn't see his expression. It was weird to see the guy in an unhappy situation, and my anger flared at what he was going through.

"I think we've got that, just. Bit of a rate hike though."

"What can I say, the cost of *living*, eh?"

The gaggle of mercs thought this was hilarious, and one embellished the joke by energising his pulse rifle with a crack and rising whine; the late twenty-first-century version of chambering a shotgun round.

"It'll be a few minutes to get that up from the refinery, then we can all get back to our day, yeah?" said Elvis in a conciliatory tone, trying hard to keep everything under control.

"Why the rush old timer? No coffee? Hospitality out of

fashion out here?"

He pushed past Elvis and walked down to the rest of The Cool, his bondage buddies and a couple of dominatrices following along.

"Speaking of going out of fashion, get a load of this one! Haw haw haw!"

He'd stopped in front of the fully tye-dyed and utterly lethal Layla and unholstered a beefy-looking beam pistol.

"Oh, *fudgemuffins*." I whispered.

Coop was already moving, quietly, quickly, head down and using The Cool like jungle cover.

"Hey baby, ever made it with a bald guy? We've got…"

As his hand reached her boob, Layla, in one fluid motion, kicked him in the balls with the force of a donkey, punched him in the throat with the speed of a striking cobra, jumped up, *high,* smashed his jaw out of its socket with her knee while simultaneously hooking a leg around his neck and swinging around it until she was on his shoulders, legs locked around his neck. She then flung her whole body backwards, taking his *very* surprised-looking head along for the ride with a sickening crunch. Then he was on his back in a choking leg/neck lock, Layla smashing her elbow repeatedly into a face that now looked like a bowl of pasta and meatballs.

This happened so quickly that the mercs, who had only just begun to raise their weapons, were still blindsided when Coop exploded out of The Cool like the velociraptor he was, landing a flying headbutt down into the nose of the rifle-carrying gimplord nearest to him. As he collapsed to his knees, face awash with blood from his ruined nose, Coop simply took the almost proffered, pre-energised weapon out of his hands and blew a hole through the forehead of the dominatrix who was unlucky to be the quickest on the draw, her beam pistol now levelled at The Cool.

"Stay still! Drop your weapons!", I shouted, very sharply,

and very loudly.

The remaining mercs were statues, the clatter of their guns on the perforated metal walkway deafening in the sudden silence.

The Cool were looking at each other, stunned and utterly appalled at the carnage that had appeared around them in the space of a few seconds. Elvis looked about a million years old.

I walked forward, weaving my way through the crowd. I could tell the lead merc was still alive, for now, as there were blood bubbles frothing noisily from the crater of his face. Layla was disentangling herself from his limp form and sorting her hair out, a slightly sad, resigned look on her face.

"Hey Layla," I said quietly as I passed.

"Hey Jimbo."

I came up beside Cooper, who was covering the three standing mercs with the pulse rifle. The one he'd head smashed was out for the count, and I looked down and saw the wide-open eyes of the merc woman he'd shot, the pencil-sized hole in her forehead still smoking.

"She had a gun," said Coop, quietly. His usually solid conviction re. his use of force blowing in the wind. Belt cops, even nutters like Cooper, didn't kill people. We did what we could with non-lethal force, always had done, and that principle eventually ground its way into our core DNA. Even if some of us sometimes wished it were otherwise.

"She did. They all did, but listen, you *saw* what was going down here, it wasn't about to get any prettier. They messed with the wrong people this time and paid the price, so this is on them, not us."

"Yeah. Well…"

I picked up one of the beam pistols the mercs had dropped.

*Safety off, high power,* I noted.

"I got these Coop," I said, nodding my head back towards Layla. He paused for a moment, then walked back towards the now murmuring crowd.

Ali came up beside me.

"Jeeping fuck boss," she said.

"Yes, that *was* a bit dramatic wasn't it."

I saw a bundle of looped cable ties on one of the mercs belts.

"Train…," I began, then thought for a few seconds.

"Part four, section sixteen of the CA enforcement statutes details the role of officers in times of war or mass civil unrest," I looked at her, unsmiling, "a distinction you may be aware of due to previous *experience*."

She gave me the eyebrows of '*What the fuck?*'

"Subsection three point seven details situations where field promotions may be conferred on CA staff, and who may confer said promotions. Given the state of civil unrest we find ourselves in, given my rank as an officer first class, and given that you are, as a trainee, a recognised member of CA staff, I hereby confer on you, Alison Drexler, the rank of probationary CA enforcement officer, third class. Congratulations."

She looked at me with wide eyes, mouth trying to say something but failing.

"Officer Drexler; these four belters are accused of sedition, extortion with menaces, possession of prohibited weapons in a public place, and…that'll do for now. Please detain them and read them their rights. The leather joy-boy I'm pointing at with this *safety off, high power setting* beam pistol appears to have a supply of cable ties, bondage games for the use of. I'm sure he won't mind us using a few."

Ali smiled me a smile that made a difficult day a bit better.

"No problem, boss."

"Fucking Belt cops," snarled one of the mercs.

## Chapter 13

Once I'd overseen Ali cuffing the mercs, who we left secured to the walkway railings for now, I checked in on Coop and Layla, who had put the lead merc in the recovery position, secured around the middle by one of his bondage bandoliers. *Came in handy after all.*

They were talking quietly off to one side, and I didn't disturb them. Maybe they were discussing the relative merits of head to nose vs elbow to nose.

I went over to Elvis through the now thinned crowd of The Cool, people wandering away from the scene in ones and twos. He was trying to comfort some of the more affected Cool with his usual, but now subdued words of wisdom.

"Hey man," he greeted me. I noticed how many creases in his face were missing when he didn't smile.

"Elvis. I'm so, so…"

He held up his hand, eyes closed.

"Don't Jim. I wasn't born this way, you know. I saw a lot of the world and a lot of bad things before I founded Gracelands. Really, that was *why* I founded it."

He paused and looked around.

"These assholes didn't come here looking for you. They came to rob us, and worse. You stopped them. *Protect, cherish and serve,* isn't that your rap?"

"Yes. It is. But this," I gestured at the mercs live, dead and beaten to a pulp, "is a bit out of our comfort zone. From the looks on some of The Cool, it's in a comfort zone from another galaxy for them."

"I hear you, brother, but The Cool shall prevail. A lot of them have seen some dark stuff too, they're stronger than you think, just a bit shocked is all."

He gave me a proper Elvis smile, and not for the first time that day, I felt a bit better.

Cooper wandered over, pulse rifle slung across his back.

"Elvis, Jimbo."

"Hey Coop," I said, "how's Layla?"

"Realigning her chakras, but at peace with herself."

"Right. And you?"

"Muh."

Coop still looked pretty rattled. I gently led him away and let Elvis get on with tending his flock.

"Listen, the way things stand, I thought it was a good idea to give Ali a field promotion to probationary Belt cop."

He looked over at the immobilised mercs. Ali had removed all their harnesses and was playing *'what does this button do?'* with various items of weaponry in their terrified faces.

Coop nodded his approval, "She's got the right stuff. Good call."

"Yeah. We should clear the freighter, make sure nobody else is onboard. On point?"

He unslung and energised his pulse rifle.

"I was born on point."

\*\*\*\*\*

I don't know how many stations they'd called at previously, but the freighter holds were stuffed with refined precious metals and high-value engineering stock, as well as random personal items. It seemed the 'tax collectors' really were little more than robbers, a story that opened up all the more when we found the galley inhabited by a cook from our sector station, the 77th.

Despite our Cooloflage, he instantly recognised Coop.

"It's fish fingers, peas and mashed potatoes. Why are you

dressed like that? Nice scarf, by the way, I like how…"

"We've got six mercs outside in varying states of health; are there any more on the ship?" I said, not wishing any more surprises for the day.

He thought for a second and said, "No, that's all of them. Dead?"

"One, two hurt, one *really* badly."

Coop puffed up with pride.

"Well, *that* is the best news I've heard for a while. Hah!"

We came off the ship and as he caught sight of Ali he shouted, "Hey! It's the Food-o-tron 5000!"

Ali squealed and ran to give him a hug.

Feeling a bit left out, I said, "Now that you've re-bonded with same-meal-for-four-years savant and intestinal-parasite-host girl, can you tell us anything about what's going on in the belt? How many cops escaped? Did they capture many?"

"I can tell you what's going on in the Belt, but hang on a second."

He removed Ali's arms from his portly midriff and approached the kneeling mercs, their hands secured to a rail behind them. He stopped at a guy with lank, black hair, eyes glaring up with hostility, and stood hands on hips for a second, shaking his head.

He then hoofed him in the nuts so hard he lifted off the floor a little, then bent over in retching agony, only his cuffed hands keeping him vaguely upright.

"My shepherd's pie is *not* bland, you arrogant prick. It is *comforting* and *nourishing*."

"This fuckwad called your shepherd's pie *bland*?" said a suddenly incandescent Ali, stepping forward and lifting the merc's head up with a handful of hair. "It is *rich*," right cross, "*satisfying*," another, "a*nd…*"

"…and I think he's got the message, officer Drexler," I said, putting a restraining hand on a cocked right uppercut.

"Mnerr…fucking fucker…."

Coop and the cook were both practically *glowing*, and Kevin, who was standing over by Elvis looked appalled and judging from his stance, somewhat engorged.

"You, cook…", I said pointing at him.

"I've got a name you know."

"Right. What is it?"

"Cook. David Cook."

"That's what I said!"

He just folded his arms and harrumphed at me.

I steadied my breathing and said, "David. What's going on in the Belt? We hear the radio, and it sounds like business as usual, but this…", I gestured to the rapidly deteriorating mercs.

"It's all over the Belt. They must have the radio stations at gunpoint, 'cause every place I've been with these scumbags has been the same - robbing, beating up, worse. Heard a lot of gunfire sometimes, screaming. They're not cops, that's for sure. Just taking whatever they want, when they want."

"Fuck." Coop and I exchanged glances, and I could see some of the regrets for taking out the merc sliding off him.

The cook was looking at the two remaining unhurt mercs like he wanted to give them another food appreciation class, and I was tempted to let him.

"How do you know it's all over the Belt? Maybe this lot is just…"

"It's everywhere. They let me off to buy supplies and I get the gossip. The FBA has taken over everything, acting like kings. People are scared shitless."

"And the Cops?"

"Don't know. The ones on the 77th put up a fight, but mostly we all went down with narco gas. When we came round, there was only the service staff around, I got taken off the station soon after. Not heard anything about the patrols."

"Anything from ELM?"

"From what I hear, some harsh words but the same old worry we'll start throwing rocks down the gravity well. I know trade is still going on as usual, there was a MarsCorp bulk carrier unloading the other week at R45-K, looked like it had cargo waiting outbound too. Business is business I guess, why should they care what happens to us?"

I thought for a few seconds.

"And if the patrols made it somewhere. If the Cops made a fight back, how'd you think the Belt would react?"

He seemed surprised at the question.

"They'd be behind them, totally. But…"

I smiled at him.

He looked at Cooper, who nodded.

"We heard something else on the radio the other day," I said.

## Chapter 14

We secured our prisoners in a cargo pod. The lead merc was drifting in and out of consciousness, and one of The Cool turned up with a medical kit.

"Whoah. Someone reverse a cargo loader over him?"

"Something like that," I said, "hazards of space travel."

I left Ali to keep an eye on things, after a brief chat about a Belt cop's duty of care with prisoners. As I walked away I turned, pointed and said, "....and I mean it."

"Sure thing, boss," she replied with a thumbs up and comedic wink.

"No, I *really mean it*."

"Of *course* you do, I got this," another massive wink.

I sighed and left her to it. Maybe assigning Coop to her weapons training hadn't been the best of ideas after all.

*****

I found Cooper outside Layla's yurt, practising disassembling and reassembling his new pulse rifle. Layla was in the full lotus position, reassembling her chakras and didn't seem one bit jealous of the new love interest.

"Well, that was interesting," I said, taking a seat on the grass beside him, taking in the peaceful scene around me.

He grunted and continued his work.

"It's so nice here. Easy to forget there's bad stuff outside sometimes. Bit of a rude awakening when it comes calling though."

"That's why I live in a state of catlike readiness," said Coop, sighting along a lasing rod, frowning and setting to polishing it some more, "you can't be surprised if you see the world as intrinsically hostile," he blew a speck of dust off and added, "which it demonstrably *is*."

I knew better than to go down the path he was leading me.

"So, what are we going to do about this hostile world?"

He put his work down onto the blanket he'd spread out.

"I still think this Point Eden thing could be a trap. But I think we should go anyway. We're Belt cops."

He looked at me earnestly for a second, then got back to cleaning his rifle.

I looked over at Layla, who was smiling at Coop. She saw me looking and said, "Bring this one back in one piece Jimbo. I've still got some moves to teach him."

Between that, and Coop sliding the lasing tube backwards and forwards in its chamber in a highly suggestive manner, I beat a hasty retreat.

*****

The next day, I sent Coop and Layla into the makeshift jail to interrogate the four mercs capable of talking. They'd barely opened the door, before they all started versions of "*I'll tell you anything you want, please don't hurt me.*"

I stood back and let the presence of the masters of mayhem do its work.

What we were most interested in is who knew they'd come, if anyone else would be arriving, and what had they done with Belt cop prisoners on the race day takeover.

None of it was welcome intel. While the visit to Gracelands was towards the end of a long list of destinations, they had in fact had orders to call here, one of the scrotes Elvis mentioned probably selling info to the mercs on rich and easy pickings. This meant if anyone came looking, they'd look here sooner or later, though it'd be a few days at least before they were missed, at least a week if they came straight here, longer still if they looked elsewhere first. We'd already checked the cruiser's long-range radio logs before we turned the system off to prevent delivery triangulation from the relays, and there seemed to be only sporadic contact with the station, though if they got a call and didn't answer, that would be odd.

On the subject of Belt cops, they were all cagey as fuck, swore that they'd never hurt any and had no idea where any prisoners were being kept.

*Yeah, right.*

It took just a few seconds of hard stares to get them to confess there were some officers in the station jail and some more variations on *"Please don't hurt me."*

Coop didn't exactly get to play, but he recognised intimidation when he caused it, so was fairly happy with the result, if not the actual information.

Layla was as cool as ever. "Later boys, peace out."

As we watched her leave I said, "We should let Elvis know about things, see what he wants to do. I'd hate for these people to have to meet any of those mercs without us around. Layla would probably kill them all and we'd have to arrest her."

Coop smiled thoughtfully as we walked, "I'm not sure we could take her. Girl's got some *moves.*"

I laughed, "You may be correct in your risk assessment, officer Cooper."

\*\*\*\*\*

"So," I said, "there's a real risk you could get other visitors, and this affects me and Coop's decision to try and meet up with the Belt cops at Point Eden. We're in this together now, and there's no way we're leaving you to face that alone."

Elvis was thoughtful after we briefed him on what we'd heard from the mercs, and eventually said, "I think maybe it's time we went on that holiday I've been talking about for the, ooh, last twenty-odd years."

I exchanged glances with Coop, "Holiday?"

"Yeah. Let me show you something," he said, hauling himself up off the bench. We walked along the broad path that went around the perimeter of the gardens and walked along a little before Elvis struck off down into a patch of woodland.

"Back when I founded Gracelands I had a pretty different plan to just sitting here out in the trojans, I was thinking a bit more *dynamic.*" He stopped at an access door that had appeared through the trees, just poking out incongruously through the leaf litter. It wasn't locked, and he opened the door and started walking down some steps. Over his shoulder, he continued, "I was a big Kerouac fan as a young man. *On the road, The dharma bums, Desolation angels*…there was a dude who never stopped moving, made a religion out of travelling round and round on the wheel of life."

We'd been descending past fabricated structures, then asteroid rock, and had entered into another structure, massive beams penetrating rock, metal walkways and then into a circular shaft some fifty metres across, and through the middle of it, dropping away to a great depth…

"Is that a fucking *engine?*" said Coop, looking over the railings at the vast length of the acceleration tube.

Elvis just smiled.

*****

In addition to the obscenely powerful engine, Elvis had also shown us a vast store of deeply frozen stores, enough, he said, for at least a year without resupply.

"We'll miss out on a few things once we don't get the auto pods calling, but we'll not be hard-pressed. I figure if things don't get better before then we'll come back over the plane of the ecliptic, bypass the belt and make a run for the inner planets, though I've great faith in you guys. The Cool shall prevail by the grace of The Good."

Over the next few days, we made preparations for the long trip to Point Eden, with Elvis and the Cool preparing for their trip into trans-Jupiter space, safe from detection and interception.

We mooted taking the freighter instead of the prowler, but although it was indeed fitted with standard minibeams, jury-rigged to fire on manual control, we thought that the prowler's speed, manoeuvrability and low radar cross section would prove more useful in a tussle. While we lacked the components for a Coop-special death ray, and the prowler lacked the power supply to juice up the minibeams, we did manage to graft two of the pulse rifles we'd taken off the mercs onto the upper hull, painting a calibrated crosshair onto the display of the forward docking cam for a crude aiming system. They'd hardly blow something out of the sky, but would do some damage to any systems on an outer hull, or burn a small hole through if we got lucky.

The freighter would also serve as a handy runabout for Gracelands in exile, and there were a few of The Cool who were rated to pilot it from their previous lives. We had, in fact, underestimated a lot of them when it came to utility and knowledge, and the myriad engineering tasks needed to adapt the asteroid station to a fully-fledged starship were attacked with gusto.

We were in the prowler, stowing our own supplies when Ali noticed we'd filled her bunk with cases of ration packs.

"Are we hot bunking or something?"

"Ah. Right," I said.

She looked at me and slowly built up to "Oooh, no, you're not dumping me here! Nope, nerrrrp...."

"Officer Drexler *third class*. As your superior, I am giving you a direct order. You will..."

"Part two of CA enforcement statutes, section nine, subsection four, states that "Any officer of any rank, receiving an order that contravenes 'limits of jurisdiction' as specified in Part one, section three, may, according to his or her wishes, disregard said order without fear of disciplinary proceedings or negative effect on his or her service record."

"What?" I said, desperately trying to remember the statutes and follow her logic. "So? Where's jurisdiction come into it?"

"Somewhere on the outer edge of the trojans, where, by following your order, I'd move into trans-Jupiter space and ELM Area Three without the correct permissions from border control. You could always place a call to merc central, get me a visa, *sir.*"

"Ooooh, you little *shit!*"

She took that as a *huge* compliment.

I looked at Cooper for some backup.

He just shrugged and said, "Personally I'd have just punched you and told you to fuck off, but whatever works..."

## Chapter 15

We were as ready as we'd ever be to start the two-week burn to Point Eden, and Gracelands was ready to begin the slow ramp up to cruising speed. The sooner they got out of the orbit they were expected to be in, the safer they'd be.

Elvis and The Cool threw a truly rocking bon voyage feast and party, with our old station cook pitching in to serve up some Belt cop canteen classics, much to the delight of Ali, who was hoovering food off the trestle tables like farm machinery, Kevin looking on in adoration.

"Do you think if she eats enough she'll go into a coma and we can sneak off?" I asked Coop.

"Can't see it happening myself," he said over a hefty margarita, complete with an umbrella. I opened my mouth to voice an idea when Coop continued, "....and Ali said if you try to drug her, she'll peel off your skin and rub lemon juice into your bleeding carcass. I told her to use chilli powder and let me film it."

*How did I get to be the bad guy here?*

Elvis danced over to us, a drink in each hand, "Heyyy, my two favourite guardians of the outer reaches, having fun?"

"Yes thanks, just been threatened with being flayed alive and marinated in hot sauce."

"Heyy, cool, I love Mexican food, heyyy Gerry, you going...."

And he was off.

I looked around at the riotous fun being had all around me, down the grass slope to the small lake where some of The Cool were splashing about.

"I will miss this place, have to say it. What about you Coop?"

Coop looked down into his glass but remained silent.

I looked around for Layla. She was over chatting to a couple of younger Cool girls, demonstrating something that looked like pulling out a wine cork but probably had something to do with an anus and someone's spine.

"You could come back after...well. We all could, I know Ali would want to. Kevin seems like a nice kid, and Layla's... Layla."

He peered deeper into his glass and said, "I only ever wanted to be a Belt cop you know. I don't know what I'd do here if we manage to beat the mercs, but Layla...this is her home, I couldn't...I mean..."

"Yeah. Well. We're probably going to die anyway, so there's that to look forward to at least. Solves a few dilemmas."

"Yeah. I find it's underrated as a strategy. I need another drink"

"*That*, I can get behind, my old pal.

In fact, we got behind it *very* well that night.

\*\*\*\*\*

All three of us were in the prowler, very, *very* hungover, and glugging some homebrewed station coffee that our homeboy cook had supplied us with before we pushed off. We dropped by Elvis' place to say bye but he was still passed out, so we snuck off, having all said our goodbyes to everyone last night, though they were more like "Ah luv yooo ssooo much, ah hic..."

"Unnngh. Right, let's fuck this pig. Coop?"
"Jussaminuite...mnng....'s ok, it's gone back down. Foof."
The docking clamps disengaged with a clatter.
"Ooooh, my shitting *head!* Can you keep it down a bit?" asked Ali, "I can hear my toenails growing."

Coop backed us away from the dock, turning us away, the slight swaying motion prompting a collective "Wurrrgh" from all of us, and then we were pointed out to space. And pointing.

"Coop?"

"We're moving. I set us for zero point zero zero gee acceleration, I can't cope with anything else yet."

I sat and watched the docks go by at the pace of a sedated snail.

"Good call," I said.

We all closed our eyes for a bit.

*That's right space scum, we're coming to get you!*

\*\*\*\*\*

We'd plotted a course that kept us as far away from inhabited stations as we could manage with the fuel we had available. We'd arrive at Point Eden with very little in reserve, which was uncomfortable if we needed to do a hard escape burn.

We kept a close eye on the passive scanner and encrypted radio, and other than some precautionary course changes when we came near a few transport ships and a very brief and completely unintelligible *something* on the encrypted set, the journey was uneventful.

As planned, we did a hard (and bloody painful) scrub of speed a day out from Point Eden, using a close encounter with a big asteroid to hide our drive flare, then crept up on the old mine as dark as possible. One of The Cool had donated a very antiquated but quite powerful astronomical telescope to us, which worked well enough through the flight deck window.

We found Point Eden fairly easily, and as the hours went by it changed from a dull speck to a dull point, progressing to a dull smudge and suddenly a dull ball, but with craters.

"Nerp, can't see anything," said Ali, our best pair of eyes, being young and less fried by cosmic rays. "A lot of features, industrial docking points but no ships. Those craters are big though, could be anything down there, some are probably mine entrances."

"Humf. Anything on the passive scanner Coop?"

"Nope, we're at the noise floor, quiet as a grave out here."

I considered our options, though we didn't have many. Pretty much came down to stay or go, and go was a shitty choice given our fuel status.

"Well, we've come a long way, I suppose we'd better have a look?"

Coop and Ali gave a nod and we buckled in for a short deceleration burn. While we wouldn't be flaring hard, it'd be pointed right at the asteroid, so if anything was down there, we were basically waving a torch to get their attention.

Once we were at dock speed we flipped over and Coop took us in low and slow over the surface. It was indeed an abandoned and messy place, discarded remnants of the mining operation too worthless to strip littered the surface, which itself was basically a spherical slag heap of tailings from the interior. We did see entrances to workings, but they were either too small for the prowler or choked with beams and girders. The craters, though dark at the bottom, were just depressions, as our laser rangefinder found out. All but one.

"I'm seeing some reflections, but it's maxing out at around six hundred metres, definitely a void.

We all looked at each other, then Coop said, "taking us in."

The walls of the crater narrowed quite sharply, and as we lost what little light we had, I lit the docking lights, which were designed to illuminate close to the ship. We entered a fairly uniform tunnel of about five prowler widths and crept along.

After a short while, the tunnel started to widen, until very suddenly we came out into a black void, the docking lights too weak to show the extent of the cavern.

"Whoah," said Ali.

"Yes, it is a bit," I said. "Let's have a better look…"

And as my finger stretched to hit the spotlights, we were all suddenly blinded, shielding our eyes from the torrent of white light pouring through the flight deck windows.

The radio suddenly burst into life, making us jump again.

"*This is the police! Power down your engines and prepare for boarding. Move and you will be fired upon!*"

It's quite possible that we were the happiest people to have been threatened like that, *ever*.

# Chapter 16

We got the full treatment from the vacuum suited welcoming committee, who were taking no chances on us being anything other than genuine Belt cops. They'd found some real weaponry from somewhere and came packing compact pulse rifles that had Coop going "oooh!" even with a vacuum boot stood on his neck to immobilise him for cuffing.

They sat us in a row while one of the still suited figures piloted the prowler deeper into the asteroid, though to what, we couldn't see. After a short while, we heard and felt docking clamps seizing our ship and the airlock circulating.

Another suited Belt cop entered the flight deck, carrying a portable vacuum pad, which he held up to our faces in turn.

Eventually, he flipped up his visor to reveal a concerned looking face with several days' growth of stubble adding to his already grizzled look.

"Officers Byron, Cooper. Who is this girl and why is she wearing a uniform?"

I immediately realised that Ali wouldn't be on the main database of cops that our interrogator was obviously checking to make sure we were not mercs.

"This is officer third class Alison Drexler," and noticing his commander's suit stripes, added, "Sir. She was our trainee under the Youth Pathway Initiative when the mercs made their move. She's shown great resourcefulness and courage under fire since then, and I gave her a field promotion to officer last week. It's within the statutes, sir."

"I know the fucking rules, dipshit," he scowled at me, then at Ali, then Cooper.

"Officer Cooper. You have five class one complaints against you for use of excessive force. Someone's put a note on your file saying *'Possibly requires psychological intervention'*."

Coop just shrugged and said, "Anything's possible, sir."

We got scowled at for a few seconds more, then, with half a smile he said, "Well then. Welcome to Point Eden, officers. Welcome to the fight."

*****

We were uncuffed and given a cheerier welcome by the now friendly cops who'd boarded us, both from the 82nd sector. The commander stomped off after telling us to give a full report in an hour.

"Are those pulse rifles on the hull?" said a cop with close-cropped blonde hair. I suddenly thought of Lissette and really hoped she was ok.

"Yep, took them off some mercs," said Cooper, flexing the blood back into his hands.

"Whoah, nice one. We had trouble with locals on the station we were patrolling when it all went down, but we didn't run into any mercs, managed to get clear and run to a little 'roid I knew about. We busted a clone farm on it a few years back and the habitat was still there. We were just running out of food when we heard the beacon ship on the encrypted set. You?"

"We bugged out of the station we were patrolling, just," I said, "found a friendly place to hide, but some mercs came calling. It got a bit lethal."

"Shit. Still, those *fuckers*…"

"Yeah. We found a cook off our sector station on their ship, told us what had been going down across the Belt. You know, don't you?"

"Oh yeah, we know. We've actually got a few Belter ships here, we've been using them to sneak inwards for supplies, news and…", her partner coughed to get her attention,

"...the commander will have to fill you in on the rest."

I looked at Coop, who raised an eyebrow. *Operational security. They're planning something!*

\*\*\*\*\*

As we left the prowler we stopped dead in our tracks, amazed at what we could see through the access tunnel windows.

We'd docked next to a habitat built into the wall of the cavern, both spreading over the walls and from what we could see, some distance into the rock itself. It bore the signs of a hard life, and half of it was crash foam and repair panels, but we could see activity going on everywhere.

And what was even more arresting were the ships moored on makeshift pylons circling the wall entirely. Rows of prowlers, the odd shape of a non-standard Belter ship breaking up the symmetry. *So many,* I thought. *Or is it so few?*

\*\*\*\*\*

We got dropped off at the canteen and had a cooked meal for the first time in a week, Ali behaving herself and only eating two helpings after it became evident that supplies were short on the station.

"It must be really tricky for them to send ships inwards without raising alarms," I said over my coffee, "never mind finding supplies for a crew this size."

We put our heads together and got our stories straight about what we'd be reporting to the commander shortly. There wasn't anything we were too worried about, given the situation, though detailing killing the merc would be weird to say out loud. What did concern us, for reasons we couldn't quite express, was keeping some of the details about Gracelands out of the report. It came down to just feeling very protective of everyone there, wanting to let them get on with their lives unmolested as far as possible. It wasn't like they'd done anything *wrong* as such (though the size of the asteroid engine may have gone outside of some planning laws, the trans-Jupiter jaunt similarly breaching border controls, though that was ELM's concern), and there were far weirder religious retreats in the Belt…but we just wanted them to be left alone. We decided to simply tone some details down and agreed on what they would be.

*****

"Good work, all of you," said the commander, addressing all three of us. I'd delivered the report, but the commander had cannily quizzed Coop and Ali on some points, obviously sensing something not quite right regarding Gracelands, but he was willing to let things stand.

"Thank you, sir," we replied.

"So, you'll be wondering what we're planning, eh? How do we intend to take back the Belt?"

"It had crossed our minds, sir," I said. "We've heard that the Belt would be behind us in any fight, so we thought that would play a major part?"

"It should do, all being well. We've been organising resistance on the stations most on our side, usually the ones that have had some really nasty encounters with the mercs. It's been a security nightmare, as there are still informants and insiders around from when the mercs were planning their move. We've had to basically keep our distance, let the leaders know we were still in the game and let them deal with their side of things. There are also some officers who went into hiding on stations, they're helping provide a lot of intel and doing what they can to organise things."

"What about ships, sir? Will they field something of a fleet if we call on them?"

"Yes, and to be honest, they'll be packing more firepower than we will, though we've got a few tricks up our sleeve. We should have around twenty minibeam-equipped freighters per sector. That should be enough to blockade any merc ships in dock, and any mercs in space will suddenly find themselves unwelcome on most stations. The resistance has been arming itself with mining lasers to deploy on the surface. A station in sector twenty-three started to fight by themselves, but we heard the mercs just massed together over a few days, stood off and shot the place full of holes. Six hundred plus Belters died."

We were all silent. That was a horrific loss of life, even in a dangerous environment like the Belt.

"When do we go and what do we do?" I asked.

"We go soon. We've not got the numbers to take all our sector stations at once, so we're taking every other sector. If we succeed, and if we're in any shape to do so, we take the others sector by sector. With any luck, the mercs may give up and run for it. As I said, we'll have some armed Belter freighters to blockade or fight any merc ships at the stations, but our first role is to board, kill or capture mercs and secure our bases. Intel is that there are still a number of CA enforcement staff imprisoned at the stations, so it's imperative not to shoot the place full of holes. I am looking at you, Officer Cooper."

"Got it, sir. Shoot our prisoners full of holes."

The commander continued, ignoring my raised finger, "Your secondary role, should you survive the first, is to immediately commence patrols against merc ships, stop them attacking Belt facilities, prevent them from massing and generally spoil their fun.

"We're assigning officers from their own stations to lead the teams going in against them, yours is one of the ones we're going for in the initial attack. I think there were two other prowlers from the 77th who made it here, you'll get the details from my assistant shortly. You'll have prowlers from other stations fill out your numbers. Questions?"

"You mentioned tricks, sir?" I said.

"Ah yes. Funny coincidence actually. Your sector commander, Saunders, recently wrote an article in our monthly newsletter, a design he'd made to modify a standard prowler long-range scanner into a short-range offensive weapon using off-the-shelf parts. Ingenious really. We managed to liberate a pod load of parts at an engineering depot and every prowler is getting the modification. We're calling it 'Saunders Thunder', catchy eh?"

Ali and I looked at Cooper, who had turned white and was doing a goldfish impression.

"Yes, quite sir. Will there be anything else, as we've had a long journey and…"

"No, that's it for now. Get some rest, there'll be more briefings tomorrow. Is he alright?" he asked, as we supported Cooper by his arms.

"Yes, he's just over-excited sir. We'll give him a sleeping pill, that usually does the trick."

"Harumph. Dismissed."

Coop uttered a teeny little sob.

## Chapter 17

It turned out we were all in fact dog tired after being on our toes for the run-in to Point Eden, and none of us needed drugging to collapse on our bunks back on the prowler, beds being in short supply in the habitat.

We woke up refreshed and hungry, and after breakfast, we located our comrades from the 77th; Butcher, Sykes, Rainey and Simmons.

"Fuck me, it's Jimbo and dogboy, how did you tossers manage to escape? Did Coop bite the nasty merc on the leg? Did he? He's a *good boy*..."

"Beats granting sexual favours to secure your escape, you rectal fungus, how many mercs did you have to fellate before they let you go?"

"Just your Mum, you mutant."

"Yeah, she said to tell you she's pregnant by the way, but she can't legally put you down as the father as you've no penis?"

After warmly welcoming each other in the time-honoured fashion, we got down to figuring out how we were going to storm the sector station. Butcher and Sykes had been at Point Eden for the longest time and led the briefing.

"The general plan for all the assaults is for five of the Belter ships to approach as close as they can, from different directions, then fire some warning shots, tell the station that they'll fire on any ships that undock. If there are any merc ships already nearby, they'll just have to deal with them as best they can. Intel is, they've still only got minibeams on their ships, so it'll be an equal fight in hardware terms.

"As soon as they open fire, all six prowlers will start a hard deceleration burn. We're looking for two minutes from the first shots to flipping over at docking speed. We can't afford to give them time to get ready."

We all murmured our agreement.

Sykes continued, "As soon as we flip over, we go for the port and starboard docks, three prowlers each."

"What if we get fire from the docks?" asked one of the officers from another sector who'd be supporting us, "It'd only take a few pulse rifles to start drilling enough holes in us to hit something critical, and if they fire the minis from the docked ships…"

Butcher spoke up, "The intel is they're docking front in, so the minibeams shouldn't be a problem, and if they start shooting, then we shoot back."

"Saunders thunder? What'll it do?"

I put my hand on Coop's shoulder, but he didn't react, concentrating on the battle plan.

"At a range of five hundred metres, give or take, any suited mercs out within the docking field are going to get a nasty case of instant sunburn. Closer in they're going to be crispy fried bastards. It should also disable a few systems on any docked ships and the dock itself, so be aware you may have to make a fast manual clamp. As an area assault weapon, it's just what we need."

I gave Coop's shoulder a squeeze and he shot me a wry smile in return.

"Once we're docked, we fight our way along the main concourse, nothing fancy, one team per level. We come from both sides, so any resisting force will have fire coming front and back and will eventually be trapped when the port and starboard teams meet. Regarding firepower, the commander has given permission to use lethal force, and we have small arms to go around, but he stressed that any officer wishing to use non-lethals may do so. In law, he can't actually authorise us to use lethals, and he'll face a court martial for doing so, maybe worse, but like he said, '*Fuck it, they're killing us.*'"

That had us snarling our approval and practically frothing at the mouth. Coop just looked serene and at peace.

\*\*\*\*\*

We'd have loved to come screaming out of Point Eden right then like an avenging swarm, but the actual start of the Fight for the Belt was both quiet and gradual.

The Belt is big. Verrrry big. A lot of it is empty space, but the distance between the outer edges of the belt (not including the trojans) is, for human and spaceship-sized chunks of mass needing to actually stop somewhere, chuffing enormous.

While science had made some truly amazing discoveries in the last hundred years, we still plied our solar system bound by Newtonian physics, mostly going around by farting out mass, albeit very efficiently.

While we'd cheated gravity a little using charged nanostructures to make station life a little less dependent on inertia to anchor us to the floor, and we'd used a variation on that tech to keep the vacuum at bay at docking points (at least where a station could afford it), we were sans warp, without wormholes and our matter transport research was limited to a few particles that mathematicians swore were technically 'real', but real engineers just swore at.

Consequently, the operation to get prowlers within striking distance of alternate sector stations right around the belt, undetected and at the same time (for the vital element of surprise), was slow, painstaking and an incredible feat of logistical organisation from the Belt cops and the resistance.

As we didn't have too far to go in belt terms, we had little choice but to cool our boots and wait our turn to set off on the ten-day journey back to the 77th.

While she was officially a probationary officer, there was a lot of training she'd missed out on, and me and Coop set to to make sure she'd covered everything a normal trainee would have in normal circumstances.

One of the prowlers was a mobile command post, with a full set of CA enforcement manuals, network pads and a recent copy of the intelligence database. The crew who piloted it were heavily involved in handling logistics for the fight and were mostly in the habitat, so it was a good, distraction-free classroom for her.

Before the murderous mercs came along, Belt cop life could be very sedate at times, and we coped with long stretches of doing nothing quite well, so the weeks went by easily enough.

And then, it was time.

*****

The plan for getting us near the sector station was ingenious. All of the Belter freighters we had at our disposal at Point Eden had three 'tents' of mylar constructed around the middle of the ship, acting as false volatile tanks and covers for prowlers. Volatiles were the commodity at the bottom of the heap as far as value went, and no merc would bother trying to hijack a load of liquified gas and water ice. They wouldn't stand up to close scrutiny, but most encounters in space were at long range. As volatiles were usually found in the outer belt, our trajectories inwards would also look legit.

The week-long journey for the two freighters and six prowlers, with all the prowler crews confined to their ships, was less relaxing than cooling our heels at Point Eden, as the tension slowly ratcheted up and the days counted down.

The evening before we were to attack, the crew of the

freighter came onto the wired comms with a final briefing.

"Ok, all prowlers hearing me?" said the captain, an intense, wiry woman with very little humour and no capacity to suffer fools. For some reason, she particularly disliked our prowler.

*Can't imagine why.*

"Listen up. The intel we have is that there are three or four merc ships docked at the 77th sector station, and sector-wide, around twenty merc ships overall with around half docked. They're widely spread, so we should have the area to ourselves for a bit, and if everything goes to plan the rest of the mercs are either going to be blockaded on some very angry stations or be dealing with the rest of the Belter fleet, so don't fuck it up you stupid cop pricks."

"Prowler three here. Can I just say that we really appreciate your morale-boosting brief, we were actually planning on docking and going to see a film. Good job you reminded us!"

"Prowler three, piss off you ineffectual little twunt, if you Belt cops were on your toes you wouldn't have let these FBA arseholes take over in the first place."

"Prowler Three here again. Yes, we were all thinking that when the *entire Belt* was throwing their faeces at us and hooting "*FBA for ever! Have our children!*" I can't tell you how bad we all feel."

"You're going to feel a lot worse if I vent our sewage tank into your environment system you whingeing ballsack...."

And thus we entered the battle, a united band of brothers and sisters.

## Chapter 18

"Ten minutes," said Coop.

Even though we'd all checked our harnesses and weapons countless times, we went over them again. Coop was carrying the same pulse rifle he'd taken off the merc back on Gracelands, and had managed to attach a stripped-down grip-grenade launcher under the barrel. It only carried four shots, but it was a useful bit of firepower, crotch-grip normally having a much shorter range.

Ali was only equipped with non-lethals, though she was fair bristling with them. She'd had the idea of combining vom-stop and crotch-grip in the same weapon, and got an engineer to print up a couple of hand grips that could fire two cans at the same time.

Coop volunteered to be a test subject, and found out that a stream of projectile vomit acted as an *excellent* electrical anode when shot into the crotch-grip cone, giving it a substantial boost in effect. As the medics carried him off, still twitching and retching he managed to give Ali a double thumbs up and mouthed '*Epic*' at the worried girl.

"It's ok," I said, "he did this for fun when we were cadets."

Myself, I'd just opted for a beam pistol and the standard Belt cop armament. I didn't relish the idea of taking lives, but if it came down to us or them, it was game on.

We all also had some upgraded body armour from the engineers at Point Eden, which though makeshift, would give us a bit more protection than our usual stab vests.

The time finally came, and we all felt the chest-sucking whoomp of the freighters' minibeams discharging their warning shots past the station, followed by "*GO GO GO!*" over the wired comms.

Coop hit the clamps, gave us a small nose correction and a

one-second burn, just enough to rip through the mylar tent and its supports. We'd all worried about maybe getting hung up, or having mylar sheets wrapped around us, but it worked perfectly, and we emerged clean and slowly drifting away from the freighter.

"*P1 clear!*"

"*P2 clear!*"

"P3 clear!" I added to the roll call.

We heard the freighter on the local net, warning the station to stand down and not launch any ships, and then we were burning hard, decelerating to a speed where we could dock at the station. The freighters were still inbound at speed, the plan being to overshoot the station, then flip and burn hard, minibeams still pointing inwards. Our irascible captain hadn't mentioned any local ships, so we presumed the Belters wouldn't be dogfighting as well as blockading the sector station.

As we neared the sector station the port side dock came into view, and with it the first sign of mercs.

"Two merc medium lifters on pylons three and seven, we're going for eight," I radioed to the other prowlers, who came back with their own targets. Ending the mission by all diving for the same parking space would not be glorious.

We didn't see the merc shooting at us, but we certainly knew about it. A pulse rifle shot hit us through the flight deck window, and though the ultra-tough composite held together, the bolt's path instantly turning into a charred mass of cracks and bubbles, the beam had enough residual energy to splash over the rear wall and turn our galley alcove into a flaming mess of teabags and biscuits, mug shrapnel ricocheting around the cabin. A chunk of Coop's *My little pony* mug landed on the centre console, and we both looked down at it.

"That," he said, "is going too far."

He punched the switch for our definitely not Saunders Thunder death ray. We'd closed to within fifty or so metres of the dock by now, and the effect was quite beautiful; the gantries, pylon and piping suddenly wreathed in shimmering blue discharges. Two figures erupted from the cover of a nitrogen purge tank, arms and legs flailing, weapons sparking and flaring in their hands. After a couple more seconds they crumpled into foetal positions, movement slowing. Coop flicked the switch off and continued edging us towards our pylon.

"P1, scratch two mercs," I reported over our comms.

Ali had flipped her seat around and managed to put out the fire with her personal extinguisher, but the smoke was pretty bad.

In the space of a few seconds, we'd taken incoming fire, returned it with probable lethal results and were damaged but functional.

*Getting downright warlike today.*

It seemed to take forever, but we eventually slid onto our pylon and clamped home. Our home.

I unstrapped and went right up to the window. I could see our fried mercs, but nothing uncooked or ambulatory.

"Looks clear, let's go before it's not."

Coop was first out, rifle at his shoulder, following his head, scanning left and right as he advanced along the walkway. I followed a few steps behind, beam pistol in hand and keeping a wider lookout and checking for any sneaky high or low angle attacks, with Ali watching our rear, both hands full of double barrel crotch-vom.

We'd pulled the lower of the three levels to clear, with P1 taking the command level and P2 the upper. Our level included the cells, infirmary and canteen. We knew that if Ali encountered a catering-size pasta bake down there we could lose her, but that's war. It's not pretty.

We came out of the docks and descended to the lower level, where Coop did a check around the corner at the bottom of the steps. He nearly lost his upper torso, as at least three pulse bolts blew the girder into a white-hot spray of metal.

He was thrown back onto the steps, and me and Ali grabbed a shoulder each of his body armour and roughly pulled him back up a bit further. The front of his vest was smoking and I felt real, cold fear that he'd taken a bad hit. Then he started giggling like a four-year-old and waggling his legs about.

"THAT WAS AWESOME! Hehehehe, oh, wow!"

I sighed deeply.

He jumped up like he was on puppet strings, looked at the angle the bolts had taken (having made a mess on the other side of the stairwell too), yelled "Achtung!" and fired off three of his grip-grenades, each on a slightly different angle that would bounce them, wall to wall along the concourse.

We heard an indistinct yell then the *zoot, zoot, zoot* of the grenades going off, and Coop was screaming and running. I looked at Ali and shrugged, and we took off in pursuit.

Not far down the way, we found Coop covering three mercs, still contorting on the floor in the agony of 'grip. It seemed like the 'uniform' of the FBA was a coherent nod to 1970s pervert culture, their leather squeaking on the tiled floor.

"Cuff 'em, Drex," I said in my best lawgiver voice.

"Ooooh, I like that!" said Ali, dropping to one knee (which quite innocently landed on already tortured gonads) to slip the restraints on a runty male merc.

I knew from experience that interrogating gripped prisoners was futile for the first five minutes, so once Ali had them cuffed individually, and then to each other, we left the moaning gimp pile and pushed on down the concourse. The first facility was the infirmary, and we drew up outside the double doors, Coop ducking under the window to take one side, Ali and me on the other.

"Ok, we go on three, yeah?" I said.

"Gottit," said Coop and Ali together.

"Ok, one…"

"RARRRRGH!" screamed Coop, throwing his body through the doors, sending them both flying inwards."

"Oh for fu…."

"NEARRRGGGH!" screeched Ali, following him through.

I stood there as the doors flapped back, continuing war cries emanating from inside.

"FUCKERS! ARRRGH!"

"WURRRARRRG!"

I waited for this to die down, then carefully popped my head inside. Coop and Ali were panting and pointing their weapons at a group of medics cowering behind a gurney.

"Alright Brad, how's it going?" I said.

"Whu, whu…Jimbo?" he risked a look from behind his hands at his would-be executioners, "Coop?"

"Alright you knob jockey?" he answered, "Got any mercs with rectal foreign objects in?"

"Whu…Whu…", he continued.

"I'll take that as a 'no' then," I said, wandering towards the cells at the back. Finding them empty, I came back through.

Ali had posted herself as a lookout by the doors, and the medics were clustered around Coop, eagerly questioning him about what was happening.

*Slightly more popular than his last showing.*

"So, missed us then?" I asked, happy to see the first familiar faces on the station.

"Fuff, *miss* is a bit of a strong term," said Bradley, "but we're glad to see you. We thought you'd all bought it on race day."

"We nearly did, but enough got out. Hopefully enough, we're not finished here or on the other stations yet."

"Other stations?" came the group question.

"Yep, not all at once, but we're hoping enough to sway the balance. Look, we'd love to chat and all, but we've got to finish liberating you from your leather overlords, so keep your heads down here and listen out on the station comms, alright?"

Medics are heroes in their own right, but they put together what we rougher types rend asunder, and they happily acquiesced without pushing to get involved in the fighting.

Next around the wide circle of the concourse was the canteen, and I forestalled the dramatic entrance by the simple expedient of pressing the auto open button on the door.

Coop and Ali looked at me disgustedly, but fell into the standard breach pose and followed me in.

The canteen was empty, though we saw some tables with remnants of meals on them. The kitchen, behind the long serving counter, seemed to be in use, and we could see steam rising from somewhere. Keeping low we edged our way towards the double doors at the right-hand side, and this is what saved our heads by millimetres when two mercs popped up from behind the counter and scythed beam pistols across the room.

The tables were at the same height as the counter, and half-vapourised food rained down on us as we hit the floor.

I turned to see Ali wiping a smear of something off her body armour, sticking her loaded finger in her mouth.

Her eyes registered ecstasy and hatred in one burning dilation of her pupils, and before I could restrain her she was up, running at the counter, both hands extended screaming *"LASAGNE!"*

The two mercs, momentarily flummoxed why someone would be screaming 'lasagne' at them in the middle of a firefight, popped their heads up again to see what the fuck was happening, and that's when Ali hit them both square in the face with crotch-vom.

I saw both of them disappear backwards with a graceful arc of vomit geysering out of them, then Ali leapt onto the counter and just started hosing them with burst after burst.

Coop and I scrambled up and ran over to the counter, and beheld the mercs flopping around on the kitchen floor in a lake of blown chunks.

"Looks like merc pizza," said Coop.

We left Ali snarling at her dish of the day, went round to the doors and started to clear the kitchen, Coop behind me. As we went into the storage area I heard a muffled noise from the big walk-in freezer. Signalling Coop to cover me, I edged my way to the door, grasped the big handle and yanked it open. The last thing I saw was a beige mass growing rapidly larger and…

…then I woke up on my back, head pounding. I could hear Ali squealing excitedly, the happy chatter of people, and the smell of…fish fingers cooking?

"Urrrrg," I said, pushing myself up on my elbows. The kitchen swam back into focus.

"Hey, here he is," said a familiar voice, and a hand grasped my arm, helping me to my wobbly feet.

"What…?"

"Sorry about the frozen chicken, thought you were one of them."

I placed the voice and face. Frank, the head chef.

"Urrrg. No worries. Been keeping alright?"

"Oh, you know. Clientele went a bit downhill while you were away, but it's amazing how a gun in the face can motivate you."

"I can imagine," I said. Ali was being welcomed by her adoring feeding crew, Coop being the recipient of the hearty slaps and a rapid deployment fish finger, mash and pea operation.

Coop turned to me, all smiles and said, "Came over the PA while you were out, P1 took the control room, station's ours! They managed to contact some other sector stations and Belters, too early to say for sure, but the general picture is we smashed it - the mercs are abandoning everywhere and running for deep space, pussies!"

"Really? That's amazing!" I laughed, then remembered something.

"The cells…"

"Already cleared. P2's mercs all surrendered and they came down to give us a hand, there were a load of our people there."

I looked around and noted that some of the pot washers had tied up the mercs and were starting to clean up the mess.

"You good here?" I asked, but Coop had just had a plateful of beige, cream and green geometrics handed to him, and Ali had become the final part of an industrial production line of tempura fried anything, so I left them to it.

The main cells were not far, and as I neared them I saw a group of bedraggled figures emerge from the booking office, blinking at the harsh concourse lighting, and one of the figures resolved into someone who made my surroundings swim again.

"Lissette!" I shouted, and she looked round, eyes going wide and then we were in each other's arms, and then…

"Hey Jimbo."

"Hey 'Sette. Miss me?"

"You've been away?"

"Yeah."

We hugged some more, and then she pushed me away, and I saw concern in her beautiful brown eyes.

"She's fine, back in the canteen with Coop, hoovering up

food like a spice harvester. She's a proper Belt cop now."

"After studying with you two deviants? Tcho, girl's going to be scarred for life."

"I'm afraid you may be right. Are you ok? Why'd they lock *you* up?" I held her at arm's length, looking at her. Other than crumpled clothes she looked fine. Really fine.

"Ah, some twerp in a sex harness came in for a haircut, started disrespecting me so I broke his nose with my hair straighteners."

"Seems reasonable."

A pointed cough asked for my attention, literally.

"Commander Saunders. Good to see you, sir."

My commander looked a lot worse than Lissette, dishevelled, hair sticking out and heavily stubbled, but he straightened upright as he addressed me.

"James. Didn't think I'd ever see you again. Did I just hear right, Cooper and the trainee…"

"Officer Drexler third class, sir. Field promotion, all by the book. She took out two mercs just now. Brave girl."

Lissette took my hand and gave it a squeeze.

"Hah! I knew that girl had it in her. I'm seldom wrong."

"That you are sir, that you *are*. And it was *so* clever of you to think of that design for modifying a prowler scanner. That idea really gave us the upper hand. *Sir.*"

"Ah, yes, well, harumph, we all have to err, do our bit and…part of a team…so…err…"

"Indeed sir. Part of a team."

He just looked at me, jowls wobbling.

"Promotions, holidays, Cooper's record cleaned and a citation for bravery. He's earned it, believe me."

"Done," he said, then turned around before I added any more conditions to secure my confidence, and retreated as fast as his little legs would carry him.

"Holidays eh?" said Lissette, "Well, I think we could all use some of those. Got anywhere in mind?"

I turned to her, holding both her hands and said, "Do you know, we found the *loveliest* place while we were out on the run, friendly natives and they mix a truly *stunning* pina colada."

# ABOUT THE AUTHOR

Andy Perry lives on a tugboat on the Cheshire inland waterways. He worked for many years in different areas of music production, touring theatre, show bands and pop music. He also wrote bits of the NHS computer system in the 1990s. It's all his fault.